TIME WAR
INVASION

NICK S. THOMAS

First published in the United Kingdom in 2014
by Swordworks Books.

ISBN 978-1-909149-71-7

Typeset by Swordworks Books
Printed and bound in the UK & US
A catalogue record of this book is available
from the British Library

Cover design by Swordworks Books
www.swordworks.co.uk

TIME WAR
INVASION

NICK S.THOMAS

PROLOGUE

The year is 2074 - War has raged between East and West for twelve years. Chemical and biological warfare has decimated the populations of much of the world, but also led to mutations in some humans. With dwindling human resources, both sides turn to Genetic experiments that create enhanced super soldiers in a desperate attempt to survive and win. The Allies of the Free World call them Augmented and Psychologically Enhanced Servicemen, or A.P.E.S.

Over two billion humans have been killed; entire countries reduced to wastelands. The war seemed close to its end with a hard and bitter fought victory for the Allies, but when Allied forces, due to a potential threat on board shoot down a civilian transport, a cataclysmic turn of events is set in motion. Aboard that aircraft was the entire family of Maximilian Villiers, one of the foremost weapon and technology specialists in the allied nations, the greatest and most gifted of his generation. Embittered by the senseless loss of everyone he loved, Villiers defected to the evil nations of the NAM powers, with nothing left to live for but a cast iron will to destroy the Allies.

With his most loyal comrades by his side, Villiers turned his knowledge, expertise, and genius over to the enemy. Soon victory no longer seemed certain. And when all hope seemed lost, the last chance for victory lies in the hands of one such team of A.P.E.S. A single squad from Second Platoon, 1st Battalion, 12th Allied Infantry Division, but they call themselves the Luckers. A name branded on them for they are all that remain of their Battalion following weeks of bloodshed. By chance they have discovered the location of Villiers, but have just two hours before the evil genius will once again vanish and continue his campaign of annihilation. They know Villiers is the key to success in the war, and are all that stands in his way now.

CHAPTER ONE

"Come on, you apes!" yelled Corwin as he leapt into the driver's seat of a DART.

The Sergeant's stripes on his body armour were barely visible anymore. In part scratched off through wear and coated in a layer of the orange dust that infected everything in the sweltering desert where they were forced to fight. The short-sleeved shirt beneath his armour was wet with sweat and as filthy as his armour. His face was tanned and craggy, but with the look of a soldier who had not slept in days, his black hair and stubble filled with as much dust as everything else.

"Shotgun!" Vi shouted.

The agile young woman rushed to the vehicle with a cat-like speed and flexibility, but before she could reach its side someone dropped from the walkway above and landed firmly in the seat beside Corwin. He was of slender build but with chiselled muscle definition and a look in his eye of a crazy person.

"Not fucking cool!"

"Tough shit dyke bitch," he replied with scorn and no sense of humour at all.

Without warning, and with incredible speed, she punched him in the face and caused his head to snap just a little to the side. He smiled as the faintest drop of blood seeped from his lip. He looked away for a moment as if turning to Corwin, but immediately snapped back and smashed the back of his fist into her face. The impact was hard enough to throw her off her feet, and she was too stunned to break the fall. She landed hand on the metal floor that echoed from the impact.

"Harland! Enough!" Corwin shouted.

"You hit like a girl," added another, stepped up beside Vi and offering his hand.

But it wasn't done so out of friendship or comradery. She stared at him and could see him undressing her with his eyes and revelling in his sexist agenda. It was Porter, a tall and well-built man who was twenty years older than her. A wicked grin stretched across his face and a huge cigar was tucked between his teeth. He looked like a bigger, rougher, and far less likeable take on Corwin. There was always something off-putting about him, and always a seedy look in his eye. She shook her head and refused, flipping back up onto her feet as if she was almost weightless.

"Thanks a lot, asshole," she replied, but his smile remained.

A snake tattoo ran up her neck and around her left ear where her hair had been shaved high and met with her hairline. Her silky black hair then flowed over her shoulders.

"We don't have time for this!" Corwin hollered, as he usually did.

He was always the first to leap headlong into any situation, trusting his gut and instinct over common sense or logic. A younger soldier rushed up and leapt onto the vehicle. He looked to be little more than eighteen years old and exuded the sort of youthful enthusiasm and excitement that was both endearing and tedious all at the same time. He had short mousey brown hair and had clearly tried to mimic the look of Sergeant Corwin. There was no seat left for him, so he jumped atop some of the equipment and held onto the frame of the vehicle.

Corwin fired up the rotors of the DART and began to lift off as Vi jumped onto the gun ring on the rear. The vehicle was of a simple frame construction, no armour at all, and only minimal stowage space beyond the capability of carrying the three of them. Ammunition cases, water cans, and boxes of explosives were strapped precariously all over the vehicle. The two sets of overlapping rotors were spinning at full speed as Corwin banked the craft, and another two identical DARTs came into view in front of them. They too had full compliments and were starting to lift off.

Two twin-rotor blade single seat bikes, they called Hawks, were also rising off the ground. They were inside a vast and deserted hangar embedded in the side of a rocky canyon. Few reminders were left of the magnificent hive of activity and technology that used to inhabit the space. It had long been scavenged or put to other use.

"Think this intel is reliable?" Vi asked.

"It's as good as we're gonna get, and I'm not gonna miss a chance, no matter how long a shot it is," replied Corwin.

He looked over to see Harland was being his usual stoic

self. They all knew the chances of success were slim; let alone survival. Only the teenager among them was naive enough to think otherwise.

"Hey, you still never told me why you call yourselves the Luckers."

"Is there a question in there?" Corwin asked.

"Should never have brought this kid along," added Harland.

"Kid?" he asked incredulously, "Why do you have to keep calling me that?"

"Because you're a little bitch who's not made for this life."

"All right, so what is your name?" Vi asked.

Her tone was unusually sympathetic and even caused Corwin to turn back to see if it was genuine.

"Hunter, Hunter Hall," he replied confidently.

Vi laughed, and Corwin followed, seeing she hadn't changed at all. Harland only shook his head in disapproval and added.

"Hunter Hall? Sounds like a rent boy name to me."

Hunter was intimidated by all of them and didn't know how to respond, so he kept his mouth shut.

"Luckers?" asked Corwin, "Because we're the lucky ones who survived the Broadhead Offensive."

"From your Platoon?"

"From our Company."

A look of fear overcame Hunter, and he began to go pale.

"Don't fear death. You can't stop it," added Harland.

Corwin shrugged, realising the comment was actually surprisingly calming to Hunter. The journey went on for more than thirty minutes without a word, each of them psyching up for the fight. Corwin finally looked over to his flank to the ride on one of the Hawks just three metres away. Atop the vehicle was another of the female team members. She wore a skin-tight desert camouflage jump suit and no armour at all, just a three-quarter duster. It had been allowed to fade and gain enough dust that it blended with their environment. Her hair was bleached blond with red streaks and tied back, so it seemed to almost blend with the camouflage she wore. A rifle almost as long as she was tall was slung on her back. But he could not see her eyes for the slender mirrored glasses she wore, a concession she made to fashion over function.

She turned and looked into his eyes, though he could not see hers. She seemed to gaze upon him as if admiring or enjoying the view, and yet her face was stone cold with emotion. He smiled back at her, for it was all he could think to do. But she turned back to the controls without response.

"Pretty fucking hot, ain't she?" Vi asked.

Corwin shrugged and smiled.

"Can't deny it."

"Who is she? Hunter asked.

"Lecia Esperon, hottest, most badass girl I ever met. And she can shoot better than any one of us."

"Keep dreaming," added Harland.

A voice came over the comms that all of the team wore.

"This is Beyett. We're just a few klicks out. Looks like some kind of underground facility built part into the canyon, and I'm getting energy signatures from the place that are off the chart."

"From what?" Corwin asked.

"I've...no idea."

Corwin shook his head.

"You've got no idea? Shit, we really are in trouble."

"I've pinpointed a location for us to set down. We'll have to continue on foot, unless you want to get shot out of the sky."

Corwin looked at the target flashing up on the console beside him and quickly banked to head for it, reducing velocity sharply until they were skimming just above the surface. A red warning light flashed on the console.

"We've got incoming!"

Vi got up to the pintle-mounted gun and racked the huge bolt back.

Missile trails appeared before them. Corwin reached forward and hit the countermeasures switch. A scatter of smaller missiles rushed out from concealed barrels in the front of their craft. Two of the incoming missiles ignited and sent debris smattering over the prow. Corwin ducked down, and a shard of metal zipped past his head. Lights flashed over him as the dull and heavy drone of the vehicle mounted cannon opened fire.

The tracer like fire from the weapon smashed into the rock several hundred metres ahead where they thought the missiles had come from and were blasted open with little effort. But a moment later another six missiles appeared to materialise from nowhere and soar towards them. Once again Corwin reached for the countermeasures, and several of the missiles ignited when a red warning light flashed to say they were empty.

"Fuck!" Corwin shouted on seeing two of the missiles rush right for them. He banked hard on the controls, and both missiles collided with each other just a metre from the lower hull of the Dart. The blast threw them off course as if they weighed nothing at all. Hunter was thrown off the side, and it was only Vi grabbing the loop on the collar of his body armour that left him dangling from the edge. She strained herself to hold on with everything she had as they plunged towards the surface.

"Hold on!"

Corwin tried the emergency power, but nothing. Lastly, he hit the escape shoot. He looked around just in time to see it deploy from the back of the craft and unceremoniously rip from its mounts and flutter off into the wind.

"Oh, shit!" he exclaimed, as he turned back and gripped the frame of the vehicle tight.

"Brace for impact!"

Seconds later they slammed into the rocky surface and felt the structure of the Dart buckle in the centre. The bow rose up off the ground and finally slammed back down to the surface. They continued scraping across the rocky terrain. Sparks flashed up all around them, and they could see a large opening and drop ahead. It was seemingly where the missiles had come from. He looked over to Harland. He was grinning like an idiot, as if on a theme park ride. Hunter was screaming in horror, but the rest of them were stoically silent as they awaited their fate.

As the Dart was about to reach the edge and make a plunge over it, one of the rotor blades jammed in a jagged rock and anchored their vehicle. They lurched violently to a halt. Hunter and Vi smashed into the roll bars and crashed down to the floor of the vehicle, but Corwin and Harland were launched forward out of their seats and burst through the windscreen.

They were thrown right to the edge and over. At the very last moment Corwin came to his senses and fired a dart into the rock with a line that ran into the console of his forearm. He grabbed hold of Harland's arm as they flew over the edge. The line finally stopped them, and both men crashed into the side of the rock. Corwin could feel blood dripping down his face where the glass had cut deep, but he had all his wits about him now; the life-threatening situation had sent adrenaline pumping through his body. He could feel his arms stretched to the limit. Harland was barely holding on with one hand, though didn't look at all scared, despite the two hundred-metre drop.

They could see it was a vehicular entrance to the enemy's base and with a dozen craft far below them. Both were able to survive a fall more than any normal human being, but this was too much. They felt a violent jolt and dropped a few centimetres as part of the dart lost its anchor point.

"Drop me," said Harland calmly.

Corwin looked down once more to see the deadpan and look of utter conviction on his face.

"I'd do the same to you," he added.

Corwin was in no doubt, knowing what a sadistic psycho Harland really was.

"No way!"

"Do it!"

Corwin shook his head.

"No fucking way!" He grasped Harland's wrist tighter.

Harland drew a knife with his other hand and rested the edge of the blade on Corwin's wrist.

"You know I'll do it."

He looked into his empty eyes and knew it to be true. He shook his head and finally released his grip. Harland fell rapidly, but as he got a hundred metres down, Lecia appeared below him on her Hawk. He slammed into the seat behind her, causing the vehicle to veer out of control. Lecia banked hard and pulled out just as they were about to slam into the cliff face. Corwin sighed in relief, before turning back to help himself. With the weight of his comrade off, he took a firm hold on the line and leapt upwards. In one quick leap, he was on top of the cliff edge.

The rest of his squad stood there, and Lecia was putting down beside them. He could see Harland looked far than impressed to be saved by a woman, and one as promiscuous as Lecia, but he said nothing as he got back to his feet. They all awaited Corwin's words. The Sergeant was already battered and bloody from going through the windscreen, but he did not feel the pain. A chip in his brain suppressed it. He'd pay the price at a later date.

"Guess we came to the right place?" he asked them.

But his humour was lost on the highly intelligent, but very dry Dalton, who simply replied, "We are on top of the coordinates I set out, as planned."

"Not sure this was exactly to plan," added Nylund, stepping to the front and centre opposite Corwin. He was cleaner than all the others and looked modelesque in comparison to them.

Corwin looked back over the edge cautiously.

"Anyone got any ideas?"

"Let me go in, quiet and easy," replied Frasi.

"Fuck that," replied Rane. The hulking soldier pushed past the nimble Frasi. He stood almost seven feet tall and was bulging with muscle. His head was shaved clean, and he grinned like an idiot. "No time, let's go straight down there, take 'em head on."

Rane sounded simple, but he was an imposing figure

of a man.

"Let's jump in there and fuck some shit up," he added.

It brought a smile to Corwin's face.

"The dog has got a point," added Porter.

"You want to get down to this here!" snapped Rane, taking a few paces towards Porter. But Corwin soon got in the way.

"Fucking hell, get your heads together, you goddamn rejects. We have one shot at this, so let's not fuck it up, okay?"

They all nodded in approval. He finally looked down at his watch and realised how little time they had left.

"All right, fuck it. We don't have time for any subtlety. Load up. We're going right down this hole, and we do not stop till we find Villiers and end his life, you got it?"

"Hell, yes!" Rane growled.

"Load up and move out!"

They piled onto the three remaining vehicles. Corwin jumped on behind Lecia. As he sat, he felt her writhe slightly and thrust back into him, her hand running up his thigh. He enjoyed it for just a second before getting his head back on task.

"Punch it!" he ordered.

She fired the rotors up and tipped them over the edge and into the cavernous entrance. As they began their descent, they could see flight crews scrambling to two of the small fighter craft below. Lecia flicked a switch on the handlebars, and a trigger sprung out beside her left hand. She squeezed, and two gun barrels on the front of the vehicle flashed into life as a hail of fire struck the cockpit of one of the craft. Corwin leaned to one side and took aim with his rifle, firing at the pilot heading for the other.

Several shots forced him to back up before finally he was struck by a burst in the neck and chest.

They were plummeting towards the landing area at breakneck speeds.

"Pull up!"

But Lecia ignored him, keeping the throttle on and showing no signs of hesitation. They were approaching the deck rapidly when she pulled up and tilted the rotors forwards slightly. They dropped completely vertically and came to a perfect stop a few centimetres from the ground. Gunfire was hitting positions all around them, but the rest of the team laid down fire on their approach.

Corwin jumped from the back of the vehicle and cleared two metres, activating a shield on his forearm as he landed. An oval, pale blue energy shield materialised in time to absorb two shots heading for his face. He rushed onwards and ducked down beside the wreck of one of the aircraft. As he did so, a tiny fibre optic camera rose out from the back of his armour and projected the view over onto the screen attached to his forearm. He could make out three combat drones.

They stood two metres tall and carried a heavy sustained fire weapon on each arm. They were firing erratically at all movement before them. They were clumsy and awkward looking machines that could not move with any of the finesse of a human. He tapped a key on his pad and a short, but broad barrelled weapon rose out from the encased pack on his back. He tapped to target each of the drones and hit the fire button. The stubby little gun fired three shots in quick succession with barely any noise or recoil at all. He watched on the screen. The three shots traversed the cover and soared towards their targets, adjusting slightly as the drones moved. They were low velocity, but each found their targets.

Explosions rang out from the charges blowing on impact in a perfect sequence. Debris from the drones was blasted out across the hangar bay, smashing into the cover Corwin was sheltering behind. As soon as the blast had dissipated, he leapt out from behind the craft towards the targets; one was still thrashing about. It had lost both its legs and was flat on its back, still trying to find a target. As he approached, he took aim and fired a burst of five shots into its head. It was finally immobilised.

Corwin turned to see the last few shots fired from his team, and all went quiet. All they could hear now was the security alarm sounding off in every room of the structure.

"Vi, Frasi, work out whatever alternative ways out of this place there are. We cannot let Villiers make it out alive. Nylund, you take Beyett and Tano. Try and shut down any defence systems and seal all access points. Rest of you are on me. Let's go through this place like a wrecking ball."

"Hell, yes," replied Rane.

Corwin turned and led the way as the group separated.

"Should it be this easy to get to Villiers?" Hunter asked.

Corwin laughed.

"Don't worry kid," replied Porter, "There'll be a shit storm yet."

Corwin continued on at a light jogging pace and weighed in.

"Element of surprise got us in here, but there is no room left for subtlety. You see someone you don't recognise; you kill them. You see something you don't understand, you destroy it. We're here to fuck shit up, are you ready?"

Hunter nodded agreement, as they carried on down a

large corridor that was seemingly the main entrance into the facility. The six of them were spread across the space and took the bend, to find a hasty barricade setup at the far end at the entrance to an escalator. Not one of them broke stride, firing their shields as the corridor lit up from a volley of fire coming their way. None of them made any attempt to seek cover, but advanced with their rifles firing beside their shields. Sparks flew from bullets ricocheting off them and their armour, hitting the walls around them.

"Flash!" Harland shouted.

He fired a shot from a small barrel mounted on a forearm brace. A golf ball sized bolt of energy soared ahead over the barricade, erupting into a blinding level of light, with only their shields protecting them. The gunfire almost completely stopped and was quickly replaced by cries of pain from the worst affected. A few stray shots still came from the cover and were fired wildly at best.

Rane managed to get a little ahead and smashed into the metre and a half high barricade as if it were made of glass. Boxes were smashed aside as the bull of a man burst through. Corwin jumped and effortlessly cleared the cover to land in among the defenders. As his feet touched the ground, he fired a burst into one who was trying to draw a side arm. Still down on one knee, he turned and kicked another in the face.

The soldier's head snapped back, and his body was launched back several metres, sliding to a lifeless halt where his neck had been snapped. It was clear these were just regular humans - 'norms' as many called them. Corwin saw Porter had his hands embedded in a soldier's throat and proceeded to rip it out. Blood spewed out over the floor and all over Porter's hands. Several specks splashed onto his face and teeth where they bore through his wicked smile.

"What the fuck?" Hunter asked.

"You're a sick fucker," added Lecia.

Corwin wanted to say something, but he knew it was futile.

"Come on, let's move."

He looked over to the entrance to the elevator and could see both a fingerprint and retinal scanner. He grabbed the nearest body that looked intact and hauled it to the scanner as if it was weightless.

"Hey, when am I gonna get strength like that?"

"Maybe tomorrow, maybe never. Effects of our enhancements work differently on everyone," replied Lecia.

"But they promised I'd get super strength."

"And you bought that shit?" Porter asked unsympathetically.

Corwin couldn't help but laugh as he held the bloodied body up to the scanners. The doors slid open. He looked down and saw a knife on the body he was holding. He drew it out, tossing the body aside like a ragdoll. He thrust the blade deep into the outer doors of the elevator and rammed it home to keep them open. He armed the charge and placed it in the centre of the floor, hit the button for the upper of the two level choices, and jumped out; the doors slammed shut behind him.

"That should wake 'em up," he added with a smile.

They watched the elevator rapidly gain speed in its descent and finally came to a halt. As it did so, the doors opened, and all hell broke loose when dozens of automatic weapons opened fire. Corwin raised his arm and hit the trigger mechanism, smiling gleefully as they felt the rumble beneath their feet and felt the pressure of the blast rise through the shaft.

"We're in business."

* * *

"Think we can pull this off?" Nylund asked.

He seemed his usual confident self, but Beyett still answered dryly as they carried on cautiously down a dark corridor.

"Our chances of success are minimal."

"Oh, come on, Doc, we're the best there is."

"The best that's left you mean."

"Why have you always got to put a downer on these things, Tano?"

"I'm a realist. It's what I do."

But there was a devious and untrustworthy look in Tano's eyes that went way beyond Nylund's understanding.

"What are we even looking for?" asked Nylund.

"Any means of shutting this place down, just as the Sergeant asked," added Beyett.

"Don't be such a boy scout. You know how much potential there is here? The tech we could take away with us. Some of the stuff here could be a game changer."

"To what exactly?"

"Money, power, all the things we want,"

"It's not what we are here for," replied Beyett.

"Maybe not you, but perhaps it's time you all looked to your futures. This war is gonna be over sometime soon. Look at this. We have got to Villiers himself, us, a team of rejects. This war is over. Villiers just doesn't know it yet.

And when that time comes, I want to be on top."

"When this war is over, it will be a time to celebrate, not take all you can get." replied Beyett.

"Whose side are you even on?"

"My own, Nylund," replied Tano.

"How can you..."

But he cut off as they noticed movement ahead and raised his rifle to take aim. He quickly saw it was an enemy soldier and fired a three-shot burst, carrying onwards with his rifle held on target as the enemy figure slumped to the floor. He reached the corner to find it was a solitary guard who had not been remotely aware of their presence.

"This is weird," he said.

"What?" asked Beyett.

"Villiers, our greatest enemy, and he is here. And yet there seems so little resistance."

Beyett nodded in agreement.

"What's most worrying is if Villiers cares that little about us, he must be pretty damn confident on whatever he's doing," he added.

"So what, he thinks we can't change whatever he is doing?" asked Nylund.

Beyett nodded.

"Whatever he is doing it must be big," added Tano, "Without some kind of game changing wonder weapon, this war is over."

They took a bend and came to a hidden and concealed entrance in a hallway. It was clear they were not supposed to have seen it. They look at one another for just a moment and knew it was exactly where they needed to go. Nylund went forward without a word and drew out a magnetic charge from his armour. He placed it at the opening and took a step back as it blew. He placed both hands on the small lip that had been prised apart and pulled with all his strength until it yanked open.

"After you."

Tano stepped back and waited for Beyett to go through, although he looked far from impressed.

"Thanks," he replied with just a hint if sarcasm, as much as he could ever manage.

They carried on along the narrow and claustrophobic passageway for a few moments and reached a sealed doorway.

"Go through it?"

Beyett nodded. Nylund rushed at the door and smashed it open with brute strength. They found themselves in a control room with five personnel working at a series of consoles. They looked utterly stunned to see them. For a moment both sides froze, until one of the staff reached for a side arm. Nylund quickly double tapped the first and then proceeded to the rest with incredible precision and speed. Five bodies lay before them and not a shot had been returned their way.

"Impressive," stated Tano.

Though it was clear he was being sarcastic.

* * *

"Go!" yelled Corwin.

They leapt onto the cables of the elevator shaft and slid down at rapid speed. Corwin landed in front of two separate fires and absolute chaos. Several soldiers were attempting to put out the flames. Others attended to the wounded, but he went forward without mercy. He took aim at the first who was unarmed and attending a casualty, firing without a thought. Porter landed beside him a second later and opened fire with a wicked grin on his face. Harland seemed to do just the same. Lecia dropped down so close beside him she was almost shoulder to shoulder. He expected some remorse and empathy from her, but it never came.

All those before them lay dead, and Corwin could not feel any sympathy for them, only a sadness that his own team appeared to be cold hearted in every action they carried out. He hated the enemy, and had every reason to do so, but he never wanted his friends to share his bitterness. Just one cry of pain rang out from one of the wounded, and Porter soon put a bullet in the woman's brain to silence her. A voice came over the comms. It was Beyett, but it was muffled and weak.

"Ser....Corwin, we...some....here.."

"What is it, Beyett?"

"You are...but...found..."

"Fuck sake," Corwin muttered and carried on with comms, "What have you found?"

"It's...and impossible...machine..."

"You're breaking up. Say again."

"A...some...time machine..."

"Time machine? What the fuck? Say again!"

"I...time machine, it's...but a time machine."

A hail of gunfire rang out over the comms.

"Come in, Beyett!"

But all went silent.

CHAPTER TWO

"What does he mean?" Hunter asked; the rest couldn't find their words.

Corwin shrugged and tried to make sense of it.

"What the hell, a time machine? It can't be, what? How?"

"Shut the fuck up!" Corwin barked, still trying to think.

"No way that crazy fucker could have built a time machine," added Harland, "It's not even possible."

Corwin didn't know what to make of it and looked to Lecia. She was lurking ominously behind them all. It was clear in his eyes that her mind was forever grinding away, but she rarely spoke her thoughts. It was her insight he wanted.

"What do you think?"

"If Beyett says there is a time machine, then there is a time machine," she replied confidently.

Corwin shook his head, knowing she was right.

"We don't have time for this," added Porter, "We came here to end Villiers life. Let's get to it."

"Don't you see? Villiers knows this war is lost, but what if he could go back and do it all differently? If that machine really exists, and really works, this could all be over the minute he steps through. If he is anywhere right now, it will be where that machine is."

"Sarge, you don't really believe this shit?"

"It's not for me to believe it or not, Porter. If there is the faintest chance Beyett is right, we have to act, now."

"Vi, come in, Frasi, Chas?" Corwin called over the comms, but there was nothing.

"Signal's being jammed, and I'm getting some weird energy readings," said Hunter.

Corwin looked down at his own pad and saw the energy signature for himself.

"I've never seen anything like it."

He brought up the map. Data had been automatically input from all members of the team until they lost signal. He could see Beyett's last recorded position.

"Come on, let's move it!"

They got up to a running pace as he followed in Beyett's footsteps. They took a bend at a crossroads and found four soldiers approaching them. Two were carrying a heavy support weapon and tripod, but Corwin did not even break strike. He opened fire with a burst into the first. His shots were absorbed by the soldier's body armour, but the impacts were enough to make him stumble into the woman behind him. Before the two could recover, Corwin took better aim, putting two shots into the first soldier's legs so that he dropped to the ground, and then fired another two into the woman's face.

The gun crew were riddled with bullets from Harland and Porter who had kept close by Corwin's side, and then

Porter quickly fired a burst into the wounded soldier as he lay writhing in pain. They carried onwards in a cautious but efficient manner, but Rane stopped beside the heavy weapon the enemy had been carrying. He slid his rifle around onto his back and unclipped the hulking weapon from its mounts.

"Come on, you don't need it!"

But he ignored the Sergeant completely.

"Mine," he stated with a grin.

His arms shook a little with the strain of the weight, but he managed and refused to put it down. It was a triple-barrelled sustain fire support weapon a metre and a half long, with a huge box magazine protruding from one side and looked no lighter than the weight of an average man. He ran on after the rest of them looking rather pleased with himself.

They made their way through several more corridors and rooms that were empty and quiet before reaching Beyett's last known position. They were in a large dome shape room, but it wasn't at all clear what purpose it served. Then out of the corner of Corwin's eye he noticed a doorway crack open just a few millimetres. He spun around quickly and took aim.

"Wait!"

They heard Beyett scream from inside as the door swung open, and he stepped out. He looked scared, as if he had been hiding in there, and he was alone.

"Where the fuck is Nylund and Tano?"

"We...we got separated. There was some big monstrous thing."

His voice was shaky, and his face had a deep cut from jaw to ear. His rifle was nowhere to be seen, and he clutched his side arm tightly with both hands.

"What are we dealing with here?"

"Something...big."

It was a surprise to them all to hear the most intelligent among them be so unable to express himself, but he simply pointed behind them. Corwin turned quickly to see a three-metre tall humanoid form armoured mechanical suit striding towards them. It was crude in design, but thickly armoured and looked immensely powerful.

"Cover!"

It was just twenty metres away down a long corridor when lights flashed, and its weapon systems opened fire. Corwin jumped and rolled into cover as shots slammed into the group where he'd just been standing. He hit the wall hard near the opening to the corridor and quickly leaned around to take a few shots, but all glanced off the monstrous armoured suit. He looked back. Rane was flat on his back with scorch marks burnt into his right arm and face. He was struggling to get back up. Harland was firing on full auto as the monster approached, but his efforts seemed to do little to slow its advance.

Corwin drew out a grenade, primed it, and rolled it into the corridor. He fell back into cover and waited. The explosion rang out; smoke and debris blasted out from the tunnel. He could feel the heat almost burn his arm from dust filling the air. He waited frozen for a moment, hoping it had worked, but just as he began to believe it might have, the mech burst out through the cloud of smoke and opened up with full auto fire from weapons mounted on both arms.

Corwin leapt into a roll as shots sprayed across the wall. As he landed back on one knee, he fired a burst into the lower flank of the suit, but still to no avail. He raised his shield just in time to take a few hits before leaping back into motion, for he knew he couldn't afford to stay where he was. He rushed at the mech as dozens of shots hit his shield, and one glanced off his collar. As he closed, he drew out a magnetic breaching charge and jumped high over the mech's one arm, pushing the device on the main receiver of the gun on its left arm.

He landed on the ground, hit the trigger mechanism, and the small shaped charge blew. The rounds in the gun blew in the barrel and ripped itself apart. The mech seemed to stumble a few paces back, juddering slightly as if having some kind of electrical fault. It came to a standstill and raised its other arm to continue firing, but Lecia seized her opportunity. Her rifle was in hand, and with perfect aim she hit the exposed magazine of the second machine gun, blowing the box off the weapon. Corwin smiled for a moment in relief, but the monster merely rushed towards him. He stepped aside, but the mech seemed to pre-empt him by turning and swinging one of its arms in a back fist action.

Corwin's shield arm was smashed against his own body. He took the full force of the impact and was launched into the air. He covered two metres, landing and then sliding to a halt another metre further. The wind was knocked out of him for a second. He looked over to see Rane back on his feet and lift the hulking weapon off the ground and take aim. The mech turned and approached Corwin quickly, but Rane had it in his sights and opened fire.

The sound was deafening as all three barrels flashed with light, and the huge rounds smashed into the back of the mech, pushing it past Corwin as it tried to move into cover. Chunks of metal were torn from the suit and holes punched right through until its back was against the wall, spasming from the impacts. Rane's mouth was wide opened as he screamed at his target, but nobody could hear it over the gunfire.

The magazine finally ran empty, and the barrels were red hot. The mech slumped down onto its knees, but appeared to be still alive and moving. Rane approached and stood over his vanquished enemy. It tried to reach out from the ground with all the energy from whoever was inside still had. Rane raised the huge weapon up and smashed it down onto the mech's arm, and it crashed to the ground. Finally, he swung the weapon around his head, using all the weight and momentum to smash into the mech's head.

The impact smashed the badly damaged helmet in half and burrowed the burning hot barrels into the head of the human operator inside. Rane simply let go of the weapon and let it smash to the ground, turning to face Corwin with a smile. He looked so pleased with himself as the Sergeant got to his feet, he was more than happy to accept he was wrong.

Nylund and Tano appeared from the corridor where the mech had attacked them. Nylund was his usual perfectly kept self, looking as though he had not even broken into a sweat. He looked around surprised at the carnage.

"Great timing," stated Corwin sarcastically.

He turned and looked for Beyett, but could see no sign of him.

"Goddamn it, can't he just stay put for two seconds?"

"Sergeant!" he heard Beyett call from a nearby room. They followed the sound and Corwin stepped through into an observation room overlooking a vast industrial facility that spanned half a kilometre. A massively reinforced glass window stood between them and all that lay ahead, and they could already make out hundreds of staff at work on something. At the centre of the facility was a structure that looked like a round pool, but had neon blue light emitting from it.

"What the fuck is that?"

"As I said," replied Beyett, pointing down to plans on a screen. It meant nothing to Corwin. It was like trying to understand a foreign language he had never even seen before. Beyett was flicking through files filled with schematics and complex equations.

"You think this will work now?" Corwin asked.

"I can't say for sure. I never thought I'd see the day. But if there's even a remote chance, wouldn't you take it if you were Villiers?"

"Chance to do it all over again? Hell, yes...How can we stop this?"

"From what I can see, everything is in there. Someone has to get up there and stop this manually."

"Someone? You mean you?"

Beyett nodded.

Corwin was surveying the vast scene for all potential paths in. He was shaking his head in disbelief.

"What is it?"

"Ever felt like you were just all out of time?"

Beyett shrugged. Corwin stepped back out of the room and found Vi, Frasi, and Chas had returned.

"We've shut down all exits. No one is getting out."

"That ain't our problem, anymore," replied Corwin, "No time to explain. All you need to know is Villiers has built himself a time machine, and our window to stop him from using it could close any minute."

"What the fuck? You're joking?"

"Fuck no, I wish I was. No time to plan this. Teams stay as before, except for Harland, you go with Beyett and go left. Vi, you're taking the right side. Rest of us, we're going down the middle. At all costs someone has to make it to that machine and stop it. Beyett can do it, anyone else, just hit it with everything you've got."

"That's the plan? That's it?" Nylund asked in amazement.

Corwin nodded and turned back to the control room where they had just been. He pulled out a charge, placed it in the centre of the window, and stepped back to the door.

"Ready?" he asked them all.

But he didn't wait for a response. He tapped the trigger button on his pad, and the charge ignited with a short and sharp blast. Inside a half-metre hole had been blown through the thick armoured glass. Cracks stretched out from the breach. He lifted his rifle and fired a burst all around the hole, and then just ran and jumped for the opening. He smashed through the glass with no finesse at all, but with great speed and power. He made several metres but then crashed down onto a panicked soldier, crushing him flat. The man struggled to get to his rifle, but it was jammed between the two of them. Corwin put a hand around the man's chin and snapped his neck. He was back on his feet in seconds and rushing onwards.

"Keep moving!" he screamed.

They were rushing through banks of five-metre high tanks resembling capacitors of some sort or another. Two soldiers stepped out ahead of them in a futile attempt to slow their advance, but it was useless. They got off just a few pointless shots before being riddled with bullets from Corwin and Porter. As the bodies fell, Corwin dropped his magazine and slammed in a new one without even breaking stride.

As the main team smashed their way down the centre of the vast facility, the more nimble an agile Vi, Frasi, and Chas leapt across the tops of industrial like structures of the right flank. They seemed to move effortlessly from one to another, and able to leap several metres as if they were doing little more than walking. They barely fired a shot as they made rapid progress, only engaging those directly in their way.

On the left flank, Nylund fought to keep at the head of their assault and seize the glory for himself; Harland was close behind. They took a corner to find three unarmed enemy staff members wearing lab coats. Nylund hesitated; his obsession with chivalrous intentions would not let him pull the trigger. But Harland had no such reservations and opened up on fully automatic, gunning them down in seconds. Nylund looked at him in horror, but there had been no time to stop him, and Harland showed no sign of remorse.

"They were unarmed," stated Nylund.

"They were the enemy. Wretches of this world."

Harland suddenly turned quickly and raised his rifle as if to shoot Nylund, who was shocked and too slow to respond. Three shots rang out, and Nylund saw an enemy soldier drop to the floor behind him.

"You worry too much about who you shouldn't kill, and not enough about those you should," Harland stated coldly, "You weren't born for this. You never had the stomach for it."

Nylund looked to Tano and Beyett for some assurance, but he didn't get it. Harland's sadistic character only proved to entertain the meddling and always devious Tano, and Beyett was too single-mindedly focused on their mission to let anything get in the way.

"Come on, we have a job to do," added Beyett.

Harland quickly led the way, and Nylund sheepishly followed.

"Just think of the things we could achieve with this machine," said Tano.

"Nobody should meddle with time travel, ever. We have no understanding of the power or effects that a single change of events could have. This must be shut down and destroyed forever."

Tano looked disappointed and frustrated by the prospect, and Beyett could see in his eyes his mind and imagination going wild with ideas.

"Don't play with fire," added Beyett.

"Why on earth not, it is fun, is it not?"

Beyett could see he wasn't joking, and that worried him, but there was nothing he could do or say at this stage. Gunfire suddenly hit all around them, and they rushed to the sidewalls for cover. It was coming from above, and Harland could see two soldiers firing at them from a well-protected gantry. He smiled as he took aim with his rifle and flicked it over to the under slung high explosive grenade launcher. He squeezed the trigger without any hesitation, and the low velocity grenade struck the underside of the gantry. It ignited with a violent blast, and part of the structure collapsed. The surviving soldier was thrown out as a large piece of the flooring dropped towards them.

Harland looked down just in time to see the piece of

walkway smash into the structure above Beyett and then topple and collapse onto him before he could give any warning. The wounded man smashed into the ground beside the wreckage, and both of his legs broke on impact. He was screaming in agony, but Harland simply fired two shots into his head before rushing to the wreckage covering Beyett.

"Fuck sake, Harland, you're a goddamn loose cannon."

But Harland said nothing. He took hold of the section of gantry and yanked it away. The hulking piece of metal was thrown aside with little resistance and smashed into the base of the opposing side of the walkway not far from Tano. He looked unbothered by the entire situation and smirked just a little, realising Beyett was out of action; and that presented an interesting opportunity for him.

Nylund knelt down beside Beyett. His helmet was almost cracked in half, and blood was streaming down his head. There was also a deep wound in his upper right arm. He felt for a pulse and was relieved to find he was still alive. He pulled out a small spray can and sprayed it over the wound on the arm. It was immediately sealed. He went to remove the helmet but was interrupted.

"Keep moving."

"He needs help," pleaded Nylund.

"We all need help, but sometimes you just have to help yourself. Let's go."

Nylund shook his head and hauled the unconscious Beyett onto his shoulder. Harland shook his head in distain; he wanted every one of them at their full combat potential, but he wasn't willing to fight it.

* * *

35

Corwin reached a sealed doorway and could see the glimmer of a shield rising up to the ceiling above it.

"Only way is through," he muttered to himself.

He placed charges at the four corners where the locking mechanisms were, stepping back a few places and hitting the ignition. The controlled charges worked perfectly, and the door buckled slightly on its mountings. He went right back to it and hauled it open with all his strength. To his surprise he found himself looking at the armoured abdominals of a monster of a man. He was almost as tall as the ceiling of the hallway. Before he could react, the man grabbed him by his body armour and launched him into the corridor.

Lecia lifted her rifle to take a shot, but the man hit a button inside the corridor, and a blast door slammed shut between them. Her shot ricocheted from the entrance.

"Wyatt," she screamed in desperation.

Corwin was flying through the air as if he had been launched out of a cannon. He flew several metres at such high velocity, and in shock, that he could not land safely. He tumbled to the ground and landed on his rifle, breaking it clean in half. He tried to get back to his feet as quickly as possible, drawing his side arm as he did so, but he felt his attacker grab the barrel and deliver a vicious knee into his stomach. It launched him back against the bulkhead. The power of the strike meant he couldn't hold on to his weapon, but he at least managed to stay on his feet.

He quickly carried on to move out through an opening to get some space. He was in some sort of laboratory now. Complex mechanical equipment that he did not recognise lay all about. His attacker stepped out from the dark corridor into the well-lit room, and he instantly recognised the hulking man.

Robak, he thought as he felt his pulse race.

He'd only ever seen photos of the behemoth of a man, the only survivor of Villiers' attempts to create super soldiers to battle the A.P.E.S. It had been too little, too late. Nonetheless, he stood a metre taller than Corwin and would even dwarf Rane by some measure.

"You're one big fucker," he said as calmly as he could and began circling his huge opponent. His muscles were vast and bulging in every direction. He looked so freakishly huge it was beyond belief. To the level that much of his uniform was unintentionally skin tight. He wore thin body armour that flexed and moved with his body, the likes Corwin could only dream of. Robak had no hair on his head at all, and the muscles on his neck were broader than the width of his head.

"You know how many of you apes I've crushed with these hands?" he asked, clenching his fists.

His voice was incredibly deep and powerful, and it was clear he enjoyed killing his enemies in a personal and physical manner. Corwin wasn't used to being thrown around by anyone except Rane in their training sessions, for the enemy soldiers never presented a challenge to him physically.

"You will never leave this room alive," said Robak.

But Corwin smiled, knowing it would infuriate the brutish man.

"You're too ugly to win this."

Robak rushed at him with a surprised turn of speed. As he did so, Corwin drew out his knife and spun out from Robak's charge, thrusting his blade into his flank. The blade drove deep but became stuck, and Corwin lost his grip as he passed by. Robak snapped around to face him and drew out the blade from his own body. Blood seeped from the wound, and yet he seemed completely unaffected by it. He threw the blade aside and smiled in defiance.

"I'm going to enjoy ending your life."

"Bring it on," said Corwin.

* * *

"Come on, we have to get this open!" Lecia pleaded.

It was the only time any of them had seen her genuinely concerned for anything or anyone. Porter set charges all around the door and blew them. Holes were ripped out of the heavy steel structure, but there seemed little hope of getting through. Rane returned carrying a huge steel bar. He drove it into one of the holes of the door where it met the frame and prised it in like a crowbar. He pushed his huge weight and all of his strength against the bar and got just the slightest of movement, but it was enough to give them hope.

"Help me!" he growled, all the muscles in his body straining under the load. Porter and Hunter got on board and gave it everything they could. Finally, a crack was appearing.

"Just a little more!" Lecia yelled.

Rane screamed as he gave it everything he could. The gap didn't look big enough for any human to get through, but Lecia threw down her rifle and slipped through just as Rane lost his grip, and the door slammed shut. None of them knew whether she had made it or had been crushed alive; all they could do was wait and hope. A few seconds past, and there was nothing, then suddenly the door began to open and got just a half metre before jamming. Rane jumped to the gap and heaved it open another half metre, stepping through to see Lecia was already rushing onwards without them.

"Wait!" he called out, running after her with the others close behind. Hunter was carrying Lecia's rifle. She was sprinting to Corwin's side with nothing more than her pistol in hand. She reached the laboratory where the fight had started, and it was a wreck. Chairs, tables, and machinery were scattered all over the place. She stopped and tried to see a sign of Corwin, and that gave the others time to catch up.

Then they heard the sound of something or someone stomping their way through the debris behind a rack of equipment. They raised their rifles, and Corwin flew out from behind the racks and landed hard, rolling before crashing into a wall. Robak stomped into view and stopped as he noticed them. Lecia pulled the trigger first and got off two shots, but his armour absorbed both. The others were quick to join in, and Porter managed to clip him once before he vanished from sight. They rushed to his position, but there was no sign of him.

Lecia went immediately to Corwin. He looked dazed and had cuts and swelling all about his face. His knuckles were raw, and he was groaning in pain.

"What the fuck was that?" Hunter asked.

"Robak," muttered Corwin.

Rane's eyes went wide in amazement.

"Robak? He is still alive? And here?"

Corwin nodded. Rane helped him to his feet, and Hunter handed him his bloodied knife. He took it with appreciation, along with the kid's side arm. The floor began shaking beneath them, and they could hear some kind of power source firing up.

"That doesn't sound good," said Rane.

"We don't have long now," replied Corwin. He let go, stood on his own two feet, and carried on. They went through another room much like the first, and it opened out into a huge circular room with the machine at its centre. Villiers stood at the centre of the stage in the middle of the room with a dozen of his henchmen. A wall of light encased them and rose to the ceiling, and appeared much like the shields Corwin and his teams used.

Lecia raised her rifle and took one quick shot towards Villiers' head, just as she said she always would, given the chance. It was the first time any of them had ever seen him in the flesh, but an energy field absorbed the shot. Rane and Porter fired a few more for good measure, but to no greater effect.

"What do we do?" Hunter asked.

Corwin had no idea, and he looked around for answers, only to see Harland step into view. It was a great relief, until Nylund appeared with the unconscious Beyett on his shoulder. He shook his head; there was no point in asking what had happened. It didn't matter anymore.

"Oh, fuck," said Rane, knowing how much trouble they were in.

The two sides were just glaring at each other. Villiers seemed utterly confident there was nothing Corwin could do to stop him.

"What do we do, Boss?" asked Lecia.

Corwin shook his head, for he couldn't believe he was going to say it.

"Lower your weapons," he stated.

He holstered his pistol and approached Villiers. He looked back and held his hand up signalling for them to stay put, but Lecia could barely contain herself. Rane placed a hand on her shoulder and held her firm.

"What is he doing?" Hunter asked uneasily.

"He's trying to talk our way out of this," said Tano.

"How?"

"He thinks he can reason with Villiers. He still believes that deep down there is some good in him."

"Is there?"

Tano shook his head and smiled.

"One day you might learn that good and evil are not absolute. None of us is one or the other. Corwin still believes in a black and white reality."

"And what do you see?"

"An opportunity."

Hunter shook his head. He was not getting any helpful responses, or at least the ones he wanted. Corwin approached the stage cautiously and took the several steps leading up to the level where Villiers stood. He looked up for just a second to see Frasi, Vi, and, Chas lurking on a gantry above them, waiting to strike. He looked back to the floor around Villiers. It appeared as a ball of light swirling around their feet.

"My name is Sergeant Wyatt Corwin. I was sent here to stop you by any means necessary. But this doesn't have to end this way. You don't have to go through with this, Villiers."

"End? This is just the beginning."

"If this machine really works and doesn't just vaporise you. Say it works, and you go back in time. Do you know the damage you could do?"

"Very much so," he replied with a smile.

"You have no idea what effect you could have. Have you never thought that things might have panned out just the way they were supposed to?"

Villiers calm turned to anger, but only in his eyes. He stood as tall as Corwin and was square jawed and clean-shaven. He wore a much smaller version of the body armour Robak had been in, and a form fitting camouflage uniform. He carried a large solid pack on his back and looked in good shape, and could well have been a soldier had he not become a scientist. Though in his eyes he had the look of a thinker, not a fighter. He was in his early fifties but looked ten years younger.

"Supposed to? Was my family supposed to be blown out of the sky? Was that part of the grand plan?"

"I am sorry for what you lost, but haven't we all lost in this war?"

Villiers shook his head as a single tear seeped from his right eye.

"I can never get back what was taken from me. But I can take everything from those who took it from me."

"Where will you even go? You cannot go back to your old life?"

"No I cannot," he responded calmly, "But I can go back just a little further and ensure those who caused all of this never have a chance to do so again. I'm going to save this world. Save it from itself."

"I will not stand by and let you do this. I cannot."

"Then you have your duty, and I have mine. Good luck, Sergeant."

The lights at Villiers' feet began to gain in pace, and it

was clear they were close now. Corwin turned back to his team and drew out the last grenade he had on him.

"Tear this place apart!" he ordered.

He primed the grenade and launched it towards the nearest console. He had no idea what he was aiming for, but was determined to shut down the machine at any cost. His comrades did likewise and opened up with everything they had. Sparks flew as they fired at every piece of equipment and machinery in sight.

"You can't stop this now!" Villiers shouted, "You're too late!"

He looked up, and Frasi leapt nimbly up to the roof of the structure, placed three charges and jumped back down, landing as sure footed as a cat. The charges ignited, and the shielding around the time machine faded away. Corwin turned with a smile, only to realise he was now standing before the line of Villiers' men, and all were taking aim at him. He jumped off the stage as gunshots landed all around him and tumbled to the floor. As he got to one knee, he noticed Beyett had regained consciousness and was reaching out to him as if trying to tell him something. He rushed over to his side and leaned in to hear him whisper.

"There," he said, pointing to a corner of the room they had not struck yet, and a thick wall of armoured glass that protected an array of machinery. Corwin grabbed hold of the handle on the back shoulders of Beyett's armour and hauled him across the floor until they reached the position. He heaved him upright, holding him in front of it.

"What is it?" Corwin asked.

The Sergeant could see a dozen digital counters and bevels that meant nothing to him at all.

"It dictates the date?"

"Of what?"

"Of how far back to jump."

"Where are they going?"

Beyett squinted and tried to make sense of it through the pain and dizziness, finally coming out with an answer. "2055."

Corwin thought about it for just a moment.

"Five years before the start if the war? With the knowledge he has, he could change everything."

Beyett nodded in agreement.

"What do we do?"

"I don't think the machine can be shut off now. It's going to jump somewhere."

"Then what? We have to do something."

Beyett had no answer.

"Fuck it," said Corwin.

He drew out two grenades and a breaching charge from Beyett's armour. He placed the charge against the glass, blowing a small hole in it before priming the two grenades and stuffing them in. He hauled Beyett out of the way and sheltered him as the charges blew. The console was blown apart and caught fire, but neither man had any idea if it had made a difference.

"Come in, Sarge!" Vi called over the comms.

"What is it?" Corwin snapped, as he still lay sheltering the wounded Beyett.

"We've got a problem."

"Don't you fucking think I know that?"

"More than you can see. There's a nuke rigged to blow up here, and ain't no way of disarming it."

Corwin shook his head in disbelief.

"No fucking way! How long do we have?"

"Two minutes."

He turned back to the time machine. It flashed brightly, and all who stood upon it vanished before their eyes.

"He's done it. He's really done it," said Corwin to himself in disbelief.

He looked to the others in horror. Every one of them had stopped firing and turned to him. Out of the corner of his eye they saw Robak appear and rush for the machine. Porter got off a few shots at him, but he leapt into the swirling light and vanished.

Vi, Chas, and Frasi jumped down between them. Besides the drone of the time machine, it was quiet now as they counted down their last moments. They looked to Corwin for answers, but he was dumbfounded. He glanced down at Beyett, but he had lapsed back into unconsciousness. Nobody had a word to say, and then finally Chas spoke up, the crazy girl who never said anything but off the wall nonsense.

"Let's go in."

"What?" Hunter asked in amazement.

"We have nothing left to lose. Jump or die."

Corwin looked across at each of them, and all except Chas were still looking at him. He looked at his watch; they had just sixty seconds left. He looked back to the console he had blown, and the dials and readings were going wild. He still had no idea what any of it meant, but he knew they were all out of time.

"Let's do this!"

He rushed to the side of the machine and stopped for just one second to check that his friends were with him.

"Fuck it!" he yelled before taking the leap.

CHAPTER THREE

Corwin gasped for air realising water was all around him. He struggled and tried to swim as he began floating towards the surface, but he had no idea how far that was. He held his breath as long as he could, eventually bursting out into the fresh air. The water felt freezing cold, and the first gasp of cool air was so coarse it burnt the back of his throat. He thrashed around for a moment, trying to gain his bearings and stay afloat.

He could see Harland, Chas, and Frasi, but no one else. His pulse was racing while he looked around for the others. Hunter appeared beside him, and slowly the rest of the team did so too. Nylund was the last to reach the surface with Beyett in his arms.

"Everyone here? Everyone okay?"

He could see them all, but knew he was still stunned and disorientated enough he might not be seeing or thinking straight. It was late in the day, but there was enough daylight for them to see clearly in every direction. They were no signs of life. He began swimming towards the nearest edge of what appeared to be a lake and crawled up the muddy embankment. He got just a metre out of the water when he turned over and laid down flat on his back, trying to get some air in.

Every muscle in his body was aching, and he felt more exhausted than he had ever done in his life. He wanted nothing more than to close his eyes and sleep where he was. But the wind chill was freezing his body, and he was acutely aware of the danger they could be in. He used all the strength he could muster to rise up and get to his feet, while the rest of them were still floored. He was caked in mud from where he had pulled himself up the embankment. After the heat of where they had come from, this temperate zone felt horrendously cold.

On his feet, he looked around at their surroundings. It was a small lake in a very flat and shallow land with luscious green foliage all around.

"Where the hell are we?" Vi asked.

Her voice was croaky and dry.

"Got to be Northern Europe. Beyett would probably know," he added, looking over to their resident genius but found he was still unconscious. He shook his head, realising how much they needed Beyett.

"How the hell did we get here? Shouldn't we have ended up in the same location as we left?" asked Hunter.

"Do you honestly think I know the first thing about time travel?"

They all went quiet and waited for his input. The landscape was eerily silent, and none of them could get any bearing on what time they were in. Nobody wanted to ask, but they were all thinking it.

As they lay there trying to regain some energy, they

heard a drone in the sky appearing to slowly increase in volume. Lecia got to her feet and looked around for some sign of activity, but the noise was coming from high up in the clouds and they could see nothing. It sounded like hundreds of aircraft passing over them. She looked down at her the console on her arm. It was dead.

"What the fuck?" Vi asked, as she noticed the same, "Anyone else got power?"

Corwin shook his head. He lifted his rifle; the ammo counter wasn't working, nor the targeter. His console was dead as well.

"The water fried everything?

Corwin shook his head. "Everything we have, Hunter, is proofed to thirty metres minimum. The machine must have destroyed the whole lot. That's…unfortunate."

"Understatement of the fucking year," Porter groaned, "Well isn't this a fucking party?"

No one was sure of what to do. Corwin wished Beyett would wake up. He knew he would have some answers.

"We need to get our bearings. We could be just about anywhere, in any time," said Corwin.

There was not a single building or piece of technology in sight to give any indicator. Corwin looked back down at the console on his forearm to get mapping information, only to remember it was well and truly dead. He shook his head in disbelief. He'd been reliant on technology his whole life, and now it was gone. His webbing had just one pistol magazine left. No grenades, and no rifle.

"Weapons' check, what have we got?"

"Not a lot," replied Rane, "Couple of magazines is all."

"Same," replied Harland.

Porter nodded in agreement.

"About ten rounds," added Lecia.

Everyone else seemed to be in the same boat. Beyett's rifle was long gone also, which Corwin would have appreciated having right now.

"All right, divide out Beyett's ammo."

"Nylund tossed him one of the pistol mags from Beyett's webbing and continued to hand out the rest.

"First things first, let's find out where, or more specifically, what year we are in."

"Rules of Engagement?" Nylund asked.

It hadn't even occurred to Corwin.

"Nobody fires the first shot at anyone, short of Villiers himself. We don't know what we're dealing with, so let's not pick any fights we don't need to. And nobody, I mean nobody, let on that we have travelled through time."

"Why?" Hunter asked naively.

Porter laughed at the kid's expense.

"Do you know how crazy it sounds? If someone had come to me and said they had travelled from the future, or past, I'd call them fucking insane, and either have them locked up or put a bullet in their head."

"But it's the truth."

"Truth? What the fuck has that got to do with anything? Truth it whatever people want to or are willing to believe."

Corwin nodded his agreement.

"We can't assess anything until we know something about our surroundings, and we don't have a lot of light left. Frasi, once the light goes down, we're gonna need you more than ever."

Frasi nodded.

"You can see in the dark? Without NVG?" asked Hunter.

"Night vision was one of the resulting enhancements he experienced as part of the A.P.E.S programme," added Corwin, "Never seemed all that useful, not until now."

He stepped up to a dirt track beside the lake and began following it at a relaxed and cautious pace. It was a bizarre experience to have no concept or understanding of where, or even when, in the world they were. He had no information, no intelligence, and no idea of what they could be facing. They reached the end of the dirt track, and it led to a well-maintained road. They spotted a house ahead.

It was antiquated in design, although not all that old. It had white walls of brick construction, wooden hinged shutters, multi pane windows, and a tiled roof.

"No way this is 2055," said Corwin.

"No chance," said Vi.

"Why'd you say 2055?" Tano asked.

"That's when Beyett said the machine was set to. Before we blew it to hell, that is."

They could see a street sign ahead. It read 'Route de Martin-Eglise.'

"What is that? French?" asked Vi.

"Definitely," added Tano.

"Okay, that mean anything to anyone?" Corwin asked.

But nobody spoke up.

"We've got company," Frasi said, "half a klick to the east."

"Everyone get down," replied Corwin, and they ducked in beside a hedgerow running down one side the road, "What is it?"

Frasi looked a little confused. "Sounds like....a tracked vehicle."

"Tracked? What the fuck?" Vi said, "Who the fuck uses tracked vehicles anymore?"

Corwin shrugged, as they waited and watched through narrow gaps in the hedge. The vehicle finally came into view. It was wheeled up front but with tracks running most of its length. It appeared armoured, though open topped, and carried a cross as insignia. It was a noisy and dusty machine, and as it rocked on by, another passed just like it. They could not see any of the occupants who were well concealed within the armoured bodies. Hunter was just staring in amazement. Corwin sat back down and tried to think it through in his head.

"Where in the fucking hell have you taken us?" Porter demanded.

"Nobody has used things like that since the 20th century," added Tano.

Corwin was all too aware of that fact.

"What's the plan, Boss?"

"We need to get to shelter and try and work all this out, Vi."

"Shouldn't we be looking for Villiers?"

"Where, and how? We have no clue where he has gone. There are no crumbs with which to track him. We have no gear to find out even where we are, let alone where he is. Most of all, we have no support, and no cause. Let's get somewhere isolated, rest, and try and get Beyett back in the game. We need him more than ever, right now."

He got up and looked ahead beyond several other houses. There was a wood at slightly higher ground.

"That's where we're heading."

"Life of fucking luxury."

"We need to just be away from any life right now while

we work things out." The sun was very low in the sky, "We don't move until darkness."

They relaxed in their current position in what felt completely bizarre. No other vehicles passed them in that time.

"Think this was the right thing to do?" asked Lecia.

"In that we didn't die, yeah, I think so."

She smiled in response, and that was a rare thing from her, a woman who seemed eternally aloof. Finally, they were in darkness. There was no street lighting at all, and that was a relief, for it would make their movement by night simple.

"Okay, stay close, stay quiet, and follow me."

He got out from cover and crossed the street into a small road leading towards the wood, without seeing as much as a glimmer of movement. He clung closely to the side of the lane and went on for a hundred metres. He was passing a small driveway when he heard a voice. He turned and raised his pistol but found an elderly man in a suit in the opening. Corwin seemed rather more shocked than the old man did, who looked at them for just a few seconds before ushering them to follow him.

"Come on, this way," he said, waving them on.

He was a portly gentleman sporting a white beard, and an old fashioned suit with a waistcoat. He spoke with a thick French accent, but seemed to speak English well. Corwin looked to the others for a moment. He didn't quite know what to make of it, but the old man seemed so genuine and was ushering them towards a large three-storey house. It was an inviting prospect, and he'd take anything he could get at that moment. He nodded slowly and walked on beside the man.

"You came from the sky?"

"Not exactly," muttered Harland behind them.

But Corwin nodded in general agreement. He didn't know any other way to put it.

"You're American?"

"Mostly."

The man seemed to smile with enthusiasm.

"I am Theodore Bossan, welcome," he replied, as he opened the door to his luxurious home. Stepping inside it was like a time warp. The floors were all planked wood. Swords decorated the walls, and old paintings in lavishly garish gilt frames. They passed through into a large living room with a log fire and were all too quick to collapse onto the sofas.

"Bring him this way," said Bossan, pointing to the unconscious Beyett still slung over Nylund's shoulder. They carried on into another room where Nylund lay him down on a leather chaise longue. It was the sort of decadent thing they'd seen in a few old movies in their down time. Bossan knelt down beside Beyett and looked for his pulse. He then removed his helmet to look at the head wound.

"Are you a doctor?" Nylund asked.

"In a past life, yes. I served in the last war."

"Last war?" Corwin asked.

"The Great War."

Corwin and Nylund looked to each other for answers, but neither had a clue.

"From the day the war began in 1914, I worked until the day it ended. Enough blood for a lifetime."

Corwin's eyes went wide, realising what Bossan was saying.

World War One, so how far back have we come?

He desperately wanted to ask the date but knew he could not risk it. Judging by the Frenchman's age, he knew they must be somewhere around the middle of the twentieth century. It was a terrifying prospect, and yet he made sure to not show his fear.

"We have been waiting a very long time for this day. For the Allies to finally return and free us from this misery."

Free you?

His history was a little rough at the best of times, but he could only think of one other time in the century that France had not been free.

"You must be the first of many more to come?"

Corwin inclined his head, knowing he could not break whatever illusion the man had of who they were. Bossan continued cleaning Beyett's head wound and got out a needle and threaded it ready to begin stitching. Corwin remembered learning to stitch wounds in survival training, but he'd never had to put it into practice.

"Your equipment, I have never seen anything like it."

"Latest and greatest," replied Corwin. It was a lie, and he knew he had to stay grounded in some truth at least, "Will he be okay?"

Bossan nodded. "I am surprised there is not more damage, and..."

He hesitated for a moment.

"What is it?"

"The skin, it is healing before my very eyes, how?"

"It's top secret," replied Corwin quickly, "We're trialling the latest in military enhancements. They make us stronger, faster, and heal quicker."

"Amazing," he replied, although looked immensely

suspicious, "So I imagine your landing did not go quite to plan? Thrown off course, were you?"

"More than a little. We're on our own out here and running low on everything."

"Nonsense, you are welcome to all that my house has to offer."

Corwin nodded in appreciation. He knew they were imposters if nothing else, but he'd take all the help they could. He stuck to Bossan's side all evening; he had no confidence in his own people to keep their mouths shut, but mostly it was a quiet night. Nobody knew how or what to ask without giving away the fact they might as well be aliens in this new timeline.

An hour went by with little conversation. Bossan stepped out of the room for a moment, and that made them all suspicious, but he returned a few minutes later with a crate of wine and a tray full of glasses.

"Please, help yourselves."

Corwin knew it was a bad idea, but it was too much of a temptation. He grabbed the first bottle and poured out a glass before taking a full mouthful. It was rich and dry compared to anything he was used to, but it was instantly calming. They continued to drink quietly. Bossan seemed to understand and accept that they didn't want to talk, and they all appreciated that.

"You should get some sleep. The house is empty, and you are welcome to use the rooms. Any but my own on the top floor."

"Thanks. Harland and Hunter, you get first watch, rotate every three hours. Stay inside, stay quiet."

He grabbed the nearest bottle of wine and headed for the door, and most of them followed. None of them had known a real bed in a few weeks, and no matter how dire or bizarre the situation, a night's rest sounded like heaven. The journey through the time machine felt instant, though it seemed to drain almost all the energy in their bodies. He paced up the stairs and to the end of the corridor where he found what looked like the largest of the rooms.

Lecia followed close behind, but he stepped inside and kicked the door shut behind him, causing her to come to an abrupt halt. Corwin managed to strip off his armour and console. Feeling completely exhausted, he simply collapsed down onto the soft bed.

Once he was finally able to rest his body, his mind again began to wander. The reality of what had happened was starting to hit home, even though they were still in the dark on much of it. He knew there was no going home, ever. The time machine and all evidence of it was utterly destroyed, and nothing like it would exist in their lifetimes ever again.

"Still alive but landed in the shit, some things never change," he whispered to himself.

With that, he put his mind at ease, closed his eyes, and dropped into a deep sleep.

* * *

Corwin awoke to a beautiful spring day. It was peaceful, and he felt almost like a new man. He got up and looked out of the window to see the town. It was a beautiful day, the likes of which he couldn't remember. But even as he began to let himself think they had arrived in some peaceful land, he could hear the sound of aircraft approaching and remembered the landlord's response to their presence. The engine noises were getting louder, and he looked up and watched three rotor driven fighters zip past overhead in formation.

He knew they were old and antiquated, but he didn't know enough to place the time exactly.

"Sergeant?" a voice called from outside his room.

He strode to the entrance and ripped the door open. Bossan jumped back a little in surprise.

"What is it?" Corwin asked impatiently.

"Your man, he is awake."

It was the best piece of news he'd heard. He reached for his armour and holster and rushed out with both under his arm. The door next to his opened, and Lecia stepped out. She'd only got her shirt button halfway up and looked bedraggled. He looked inside the room to see Vi lying naked on the bed and looking more than a little happy with herself. Fortunately, Bossan had already looked away at the sight of Lecia and saved them all the difficulty of explaining what he hadn't seen.

"What is it?"

"Beyett is back with us."

She rushed on after him to the room where Beyett had been and found him sitting up in a lavishly decorated chair. He looked wiped out but conscious. Corwin opened his mouth to speak, but he stopped himself on seeing the Frenchman had followed him into the room.

"Can we have a minute?"

Bossan nodded happily and stepped out.

"Corwin, what the fuck is going on?"

"I guess nobody has told you, then?"

"Told me what?" he replied, rubbing his aching head.

Corwin was trying to find the words to explain it.

"We destroyed it, right?" Beyett asked.

"It's gone for sure."

Beyett sighed in relief.

"So where are we?" he asked, looking around at their bizarre and antiquated surroundings.

"Thing's didn't exactly go to plan. Villiers made it through."

"And?"

"And it was a choice of follow after him, or death by the nuke set off to destroy everything that had been built."

Beyett slumped back into his chair.

"We had no choice, Doc," added Lecia; with the name she affectionately referred to him as. He wasn't a doctor, but he was a highly qualified University postgraduate, the likes of which none of them had ever known.

Beyett rubbed his head with one hand and chin with the other, as he tried to get his head around it all.

"So where are we?" he finally asked.

"France by the looks of it."

"But when?"

"Middle of the twentieth century, I'd say."

"I'd hoped we had destroyed the device that plotted a path and could have sent Villiers into oblivion."

"Same," replied Corwin.

"So where is Villiers?"

Corwin shrugged.

Beyett finally sat up in amazement and absolute focus as if he'd just been given an adrenaline shot.

"You don't know?"

"Not had a lot of time to figure it out, Doc," replied Lecia.

"It is all that matters. Do you know how much damage

he could do? Every single action he, and any of us makes here, could be detrimental to the future of civilisation."

"Whoa now, take it easy."

"Take it easy? Sergeant, you have no concept of how much of a disaster this is. The whole war we fought just meant nothing. Villiers is here, and with all his knowledge, his power, and his will to destroy everything we fought for…"

He stopped himself, trying to breathe and calm down, and then continued.

"Every minute that goes by that we haven't stopped Villiers is a moment for him to destroy everything. We cannot lie about here and do nothing."

"And we won't, but we need information."

"Yes, so firstly, what year is it?"

Corwin shook his head.

"You've got a local taking care of me, ask him."

"How? We can't give away who and what we are."

Beyett shook his head.

"Call him back in here."

Corwin did as he was asked and returned with Bossan.

"I cannot thank you enough for the care you have shown me," said Beyett in a calm and grateful tone.

"It is no problem at all, Monsieur. You are fighting for our freedom. It is the least I can do."

Beyett nodded slowly.

"I do not suppose you have got today's newspaper to hand, have you?" he asked politely.

"Why of course, but don't you know better than us what is going on?"

"Just something to pass a little time until I get back on my feet."

"Of course, you speak French?"

"I can read enough."

Bossan strode out of the room and came back with the newspaper.

"Then I shall leave you gentlemen to it."

He looked to Lecia and didn't quite know how to address her, so simply smiled and left. The two of them jumped to Beyett's side as he took up the paper and looked for the date.

"April 13, 1943," stated Beyett.

"What does that mean?" asked Lecia.

Beyett shook his head. "It means we have landed slap bang in the midst of World War Two. Not only that, but if we're in France in forty-three, we are in trouble."

"Why?"

"Because the Allied invasion hasn't begun yet. This is occupied territory, and we will be treated as enemy combatants, or worse, as spies."

He looked down at the headline of the paper, and his eyes widened in amazement.

"No way, it isn't possible."

"What is it?"

Corwin and Lecia looked carefully, but it meant nothing to them. It was in French, and even if it hadn't been, they had little understanding of the time period.

"It says the Urals have fallen. It is the end of the Soviet Union."

He looked to the two of them for some reaction, but it never came.

"Don't you see? This never happened."

"What?" Corwin exclaimed.

"The Soviet Union never fell, and in forty-three, that'll

mean the Allied invasion of France in forty-four will not get off the ground…"

He was in utter shock, but none of it meant anything to the other two.

"Didn't you ever do history, Sergeant?"

"Come on, I'm a fighter, not a fucking historian."

"Those who cannot learn from history are doomed to repeat it. That not mean anything to you?"

Corwin knew what he meant, but it still didn't help.

"Sergeant, we've got company!" Nylund interrupted them.

Corwin dropped everything they were discussing and rushed to Nylund's side and the window he was looking out of. A small-wheeled vehicle and a truck rode up the path towards the house. There was some high-ranking official in the lead vehicle, and twenty soldiers in the back of the truck. One stood atop a machine gun mounted on the truck.

Bossan appeared at his side and looked terrified.

"Come with me, you must hurry. I can hide you. It will all be okay."

"Hide?"

It wasn't a concept Corwin was familiar with or liked the sound of.

"He's right," said Beyett.

Corwin turned to see the Doc was propped up in the doorway behind them.

"This isn't our fight. We can't get involved."

Bossan looked confused.

"If they find you here, they will kill you. Please, let me show you to somewhere safe."

Corwin looked to Beyett for answers, as he seemed to

understand it better than any of them. He simply nodded in approval. Corwin shook his head. He hated shying away from a fight.

"All right, get everyone down here," he said to Lecia, "but you and Frasi stay up top to cover us if we get into any trouble."

She rushed off without another word as Bossan drew back a large rug in the centre of the room. It revealed a large trap door in the middle of the planked floor. He pulled it back and ushered Corwin and the others down into the dark cellar. He slammed the door behind them and placed the rug back, although they could still see the cracks through the rest of the floorboards around the rug.

"Hide? That's your answer?" Harland asked in disgust.

"Don't presume to know anything about the shit storm we have landed in," replied Beyett.

The ten of them were crammed in tight and could not help but feel caged. They were silent on hearing the vehicles come to a halt next to the house. Corwin pulled out his pistol and held it at the ready. He didn't like this plan at all, and had not felt so uneasy in some time.

"That old fool is going to get us killed," said Porter.

"Have a little faith," said Beyett, "These people endured a war just as bitter as the one we know. He's been nothing but good to us."

They could hear the sound of boots hitting the ground as the vehicles unloaded, and the heavy footsteps of the officers striding towards the door. It went quiet, and then finally two heavy knocks on the door.

"Open up!" a voice called.

The man spoke with a deep and booming voice. His German accent was evident, but his English was clear and precise. Bossan paced casually and calmly to the door, opening it as if to welcome guests.

"Good morning, gentlemen," he said politely.

"Good morning," the response came. The two officers stepped through into his house without being invited in. Corwin could already tell it was not a comfortable situation. He felt his pulse rising as he always would before a fight. His hand clenched his pistol tightly, and he felt a little sweat drop from his brow.

"This fucking sucks," whispered Porter.

But Corwin did not respond, as he listened intently for every movement and word above them. The footsteps continued, and through a gap in the floorboards he saw the two officers enter the room. They wore the field grey uniforms of the German military, but it was Beyett who pointed to the Death's Head symbols on their caps.

"SS," he whispered.

Corwin knew that name and had some understanding of what it meant.

"How can I help you gentlemen?" Bossan asked.

"We have reports of a group of clandestine enemy forces in the area, you have not encountered any such activity?" asked one.

Bossan sighed. "I am sorry, but I have been asleep all night, and my sight is not quite what is used to be," he jested.

"I never said anything about night."

Corwin could hear the flap of one of the officers' leather holsters open, and a pistol be drawn. It made him anxious, and it was soon followed by the cocking mechanism of the pistol.

"You have three seconds to tell me the whereabouts of

these enemy combatants."

Corwin felt Beyett's hand on his shoulder in an attempt to restrain him, but he could feel his blood boiling. It wasn't often he had known such kindness as Bossan had shown them, and the anger was causing his hands to shake with a bitter hatred for this new threat. An enemy they had never known. He had known the Nazis were the enemy of his ancestors, but it had meant nothing to him.

Beyett leaned in close and whispered in Corwin's ear.

"If we interfere, we could well cause as much damage as Villiers himself."

But it was too late to change his mind because the German officer began the count down.

"Three seconds...tell us where the enemy is, and we shall spare your life, or do you wish to die for the English and American dogs who left you behind? What do you owe them? Tell us where they are, and you may go on with your life without any further repercussions."

"I have seen no foreigners here besides yourselves."

Beyett shook his head. He knew that would only serve to infuriate the SS officers.

"Three seconds to save your life...three...two...."

CHAPTER FOUR

The floorboards burst open like a bomb going off as Corwin jumped out from hiding. The two officers were utterly stunned, and one staggered back against the far wall. Corwin took aim at the one holding the gun and fired two shots into his chest, killing him instantly. He turned the weapon on the other and put three into the centre of his body. He slumped down dead in front of Bossan, who could do nothing but stare at the brutality in his home.

Footsteps of the two nearest soldiers on guard could be heard rushing towards them, and Bossan stood between them and him. Corwin leapt for the entrance to the room as they entered. Both wore the field grey German uniforms he remembered from the movies, but also had torso body armour that seemed entirely anachronistic. He fired two shots into their chests, but neither got through. They were carrying large magazine fed assault rifles and both were being brought to bear on Corwin.

He rushed towards them firing into the face of the nearest and grabbed hold of the muzzle of the rifle of the second. He pulled it aside, just as the soldier pulled the trigger, and fully automatic fire peppered the wall of the room. Corwin smashed the barrel of his pistol into the man's face, grasped him by the throat, and launched him across the room. His superhuman strength propelled the man five metres, and he smashed into the wall above the fireplace, tumbling back to the floor in a stunned state. Before he could recover, Vi fired a shot into his face as she leapt out from the basement.

Another soldier rushed into the room, but before he could lift his rifle, Corwin drove a kick into the centre of his chest armour and launched him through the bay window. The glass shattered as he cannoned through it and tumbled into the open top staff car parked outside, much to the shock and amazement of those rushing to the entrance of the house. Then Corwin noticed the gunner on the top of the truck swivel the weapon around to take aim.

"Down!" he yelled.

He jumped for cover; the gun opened up like a jackhammer. Even as he was flying through the air, the glass of the window was hitting the side of his face. He could do nothing but hunker down on the floor as the deafening weapon tore the room apart. Lecia leaned out from the window of the highest room in the house and quickly took aim at the gunner. She squeezed the trigger, and the shot hit the man's helmet. It passed right through and exited at his jaw to kill him instantly. A hail of gunfire was turned her way, and she leapt nimbly back from the shots peppering the window frame.

"Is there a way out from the cellar to the outside?" Corwin shouted across to Bossan.

He nodded and pointed, but before he said a word, they heard the sound of one of their rifles rattle off outside. Corwin got up and looked through the shattered window. Rane and Porter had already made it through and were firing on fill auto. A grenade was tossed though the window, and he saw it just in time. He jumped and caught it before it could land, tossing it back out with such lightning speed and reactions that Bossan couldn't believe what he was seeing.

Rane's clip ran empty, and instead of reloading, he too made a running leap and landed on top of the truck beside where the gunner's body lay slumped over the cabin roof. The suspension rocked from his huge weight landing and almost caused it to go up on two wheels. He picked up the dead body with one hand, threw him out of the cab, and then took up the machine gun. The heavy and long barrelled weapon looked tiny in his hands, but he took aim and pulled the trigger.

Six of the German soldiers were struck down as if by firing squads, their bodies riddled with fire from the weapon and driven up against the side of the house. Finally, the belt of ammunition ran dry, but that wouldn't stop Rane. He jumped from the truck and cleared several metres. He hit the ground running at one of the soldiers who was panicking and firing randomly. Two of the shots hit Rane's body armour, while another passed through his left tricep. He brushed it off and rushed at the man, striking him like a truck.

The soldier was launched into the air and hit the side of the house so hard several bricks were dislodged. He was immediately incapacitated and dropped limply to the ground. He turned to see another of the German soldiers about to fire at him point blank, but Frasi seemed to descend out of nowhere and land on top of the soldier. In one quick and precise action he slit his throat with a tiny, but razor sharp blade. The soldier collapsed with Frasi still on his back.

Corwin picked up the nearest rifle from one of their fallen adversaries and rushed into the hallway as five soldiers were making their way inside. He fired a burst into the legs of the first and the face of the second, before ducking back into the room he had come from.

He was about to return fire when Chas passed him at speed. She went into a dive through the entrance and below the gunfire. She looked so peaceful, focused, and precise that it was more like a dance than a fight. She rolled across the floor and rose up in front of the three remaining soldiers. She held a pistol in each hand and placed one each against two of the soldiers' kneecaps and fired. Both dropped to the ground screaming in agony.

She brought both pistols together, fired two shots with each into the third soldier's face, then stood up and double tapped the two wounded in the head also. She looked back to Corwin as if expecting some kind of praise. She looked both happy with her own work, and high on some kind of drug. He was never sure if she was crazier and sicker than Porter.

"Feels just like home," she finally said with a wicked smile.

"You're fucked up, you know that?" Nylund asked and strode out into the corridor.

"Where the fuck were you?" asked Corwin.

"Covering the side entrance," he replied quickly.

"Enough of the jealousy, boys," replied Chas, "We can't

all be masters of our art."

Corwin shook his head. She seemed so far out of touch with reality it was almost funny. As it happens, he'd live with her craziness because it came with exceptional ability. A final few gunshots rang out from outside, and then all was quiet. There were no screams of the wounded. His team was not trained to take prisoners or leave survivors. Some enjoyed that part of the job more than others. Corwin looked around as Bossan stepped into the hallway open mouthed. But Corwin knew it wasn't the sight of blood or death that was bothering him so much.

"Who are you people?"

He was silenced, and none of them had a simple way of explaining it. Beyett stepped into view.

"All you need to know is that we are here to help."

"That is what the Germans keep telling us, and you can see the extent of their help."

Corwin didn't know what to do or say, but Bossan seemed to calm down all by himself as he reflected on all that had happened.

"You did that for me? You could just as well have stayed hidden and let them kill me?"

Corwin shrugged.

"Why? You don't even know me."

"Why did you take us in? Why did you help any of us?"

It was a deeply warming thought to Bossan, and he began to accept they were not the enemy.

"I am sorry I cannot be any clearer," Corwin said, "All I can tell you is that we are on a mission of the utmost of importance. A mission far greater than you may even begin to imagine or understand. A lot more than your freedom is at stake, and beyond that, I must ask you take my word."

Beyett was shocked and surprised at Corwin's empathy and ability to defuse the situation so well. He had no idea where that had come from.

"Tell me how I can help?" Bossan asked enthusiastically.

"You have done more than enough already," replied Beyett, "Find somewhere safe to ride this out."

But he shook his head.

"No need. The Allies will be here tonight. It will be chaos. This will be no problem."

Beyett looked confused. He could not think what could be happening in France in 1943.

"This town, what's it called?"

"Dieppe."

Beyett's face was gaunt with a look of horror.

"They're trying again?"

"Again? We've not known Allied soldiers on our soil since the disaster at Dunkerque."

"What is it?"

Beyett shook his head and would not answer Corwin.

"You must go quickly. There will surely be more soldiers along shortly. I will stay out of sight until the night, but you must go," said Bossan.

Corwin was not at all certain what they should do, but he knew Bossan was right.

"Everyone grab your gear. We're leaving!" he bellowed.

He offered out his hand to Bossan to thank him, before turning and leaving over the line of bodies.

"You're a good man. Stay safe," he replied as he headed out the door.

"Round up any weapons and ammunition you can. We're gonna need them," he said, picking up one of the assault rifles and six magazines from two of the bodies.

"Pretty sure these shouldn't even exist yet," said Beyett as he did the same.

"Changes of events. Equipment ahead of its time, what are you telling me?"

"That the only explanation for this is someone having changed time."

"But how? Villiers only just arrived."

"So you think, but you don't know that."

Corwin shook his head in disbelief, beginning to consider the prospect Beyett was proposing. He didn't want to think about it for now; they had enough problems just surviving.

It was a beautifully sunny day with perfect visibility, but fortunately they didn't have far to go. Corwin led them back to the track where they first found the house and carried on to the wood.

"1943? What a fucking joke!"

"Hey, Porter, what did you have to live for in our time?" Nylund asked.

"Yeah, you can enjoy killing in this time just as easily," added Vi.

Porter smiled in response, for he knew it to be true. They carried on for a mile into the wood, deep enough in that they were well concealed when Corwin called them to a halt. He took a seat on a fallen tree as they gathered around him.

"So what's the deal here, Boss?" Vi asked.

"Not quick on the take up, are you, bitch?"

"Hey, fuck you, Porter, it's not like you have all the answers."

"Enough!" Corwin shouted, "Only one thing seems

certain right now, and that is we are in deep shit. So let's not build on the stack of shit that is already resting on us, okay? Let's put our heads together and try and work this out."

"You're the boss. It's your call," Nylund said in a rather unhelpful fashion.

Corwin wanted to put him down for the comment, knowing he was both a hypocrite and an asshole, but he knew it wouldn't be productive.

"I run operations planned on a large scale by hundreds of far smarter people than any of us. I'm a squad leader, not a goddamn shot caller. So yes, I'm still in charge here, but a little input would be nice. Beyett, you know more about this age than any of us, and you're the smartest. I'm gonna rely very heavily on you in the coming days and weeks, if we make it that far. Of all of us, Beyett is the number one most important member of this team, so you protect him at all costs, you got it?"

Most of them nodded in agreement.

"Beyett, you clearly have a lot more to say about all this, so start talking."

Beyett took in a deep breath as he thought it all over and tried to put it into words that would make sense to them all.

"It's 1943, but not as I learnt of it. Someone has changed this time line. We interfered with the time machine when it was in operation. Clearly, we weren't supposed to arrive in this time. Those two things being the case, it begs the question, where did Villiers arrive? Or when, more specifically?"

"You're saying Villiers got here ahead of us somehow?"

"That's exactly what he's saying, Vi," added Harland,

"Fucking with that machine really did us a lot of good."

"I don't think it matters at all," Chas commented.

They were all surprised to hear her have any sensible input and waited for her to continue.

"Our job is to end Villiers, doesn't matter in what country, in what time, or on what planet we do it."

They were all dumbfounded. It was logical, even if it sounded crazy.

"But the next problem is this," Beyett continued, "Every change that is made in this time has the potential to radically change everything in our own time. Or what was our time. It is the domino effect. Something as simple as a conversation with a local could make vast changes to all our futures. We shouldn't even have encountered Bossan, let alone picked a fight with those soldiers."

"I had no choice."

"Of course you did, Corwin. We all did."

"So what, we try and go through this time zone without affecting a single thing, while trying to reach Villiers?"

"As much as is humanly possible, yes."

Corwin shook his head.

"Hasn't it occurred to you that with all these changes, he's probably more powerful than ever?"

"Maybe, but that is not a reason to not try."

"So that is our plan?" asked Nylund.

"Seems reasonable. Same as it was before, just as Chas said. We're here to kill Villiers. The circumstances may have changed drastically, but our mission is more important than ever."

They were all quiet, as they began to digest all that they were experiencing. Hunter broke the silence.

"So whose side we on here, Sarge?"

Corwin laughed. "Well we sure ain't no Nazis, but I am not certain we'll get an awfully warm welcome anywhere, right now."

"Villiers must have some sizeable influence and power to have made this much of an effect on the world, so he won't be easy to reach."

"No, but he also has no idea we are here," added Corwin, "He doesn't know we made it through or that we are coming for him. We must use that."

"But we need to find a way to blend in," replied Beyett.

"Bossan said the Allies are launching an offensive here tonight. We should be able to fit in with them just fine."

"Dressed like this and carrying enemy weapons?"

"I didn't say it was a perfect plan, Nylund, but I'm working on it."

The rest of them began to relax and sat down wherever they could, not as they they'd be staying put for some time. Corwin pulled out a ration bar from his webbing and noted there were only three more left; two days' supply in total. He tore open the packaging and bit off half of the ration in one, chewing down on it with a wince. They never tasted good, but it was sustenance at least.

"Any chance of getting our gear working?" asked Vi.

Beyett shook his head. "Everything's fried. But hang onto it, we may have use for it all yet."

"What, throw it at the enemy?"

Corwin smiled at Porter. They rested for half an hour and contemplated their situation. Beyett stepped over and sat down beside Corwin so they could talk more privately.

"You know that our chances of even surviving a few days in this war are slim?"

Corwin nodded.

"We've been through plenty and come out on top."

"I don't think you appreciate the seriousness of our situation. In fact, I am still struggling to understand it myself. You know this is the kind of theoretical situation I discussed as a student, but never believed could truly happen."

"Yeah, well, life's a bitch sometimes."

Beyett nodded.

"We're never going back, are we?"

Beyett shook his head. "If Villiers made a machine once, then maybe he could do it again, but who knows? Even if we could go back, it would already be a world we would not recognise. Everything has changed too much already."

Corwin said nothing.

"That doesn't bother you?"

Corwin shook his head and smiled as he looked around at the team.

"We've been at this so long this is all the family any of us really have. What does it matter what country or time we are in? This is home to us," he said, pointing at them.

Beyett seemed impressed.

"But tell me this. Seeing as we are now in a time long before any of us were born, can we somehow change events so that we ourselves were simply different, or never born at all?"

Beyett shook his head. "There have been many theories, but I have never been sure what to believe. Honestly, I never gave it a whole lot of thought. Of all the scenarios we could have found ourselves in, this is about the most unlikely I could have imagined."

"But what do you believe would happen?"

Beyett took a deep breath before answering. "I believe we have already been made as we are. If we could travel to some time in between now and our time, yes I'm sure we would find a very different us. But I think we are separated from that timeline now. We exist in this one as if we were born in it. Or at least I hope that to be the case."

"And the alternative?"

"That Villiers could ensure none of us ever existed? Let's not consider that possibility, hey?"

"Nylund got up, strode up to Corwin and stopped before him, expecting some kind of acknowledgement, but Corwin didn't give it.

"Shouldn't we be doing something? We can't waste a whole day."

Corwin looked up at him but sighed. He didn't want to have to explain it but knew he had to.

"There's plenty of hard work ahead for us, but we must be aware of the dangers that surround us. We must bide our time."

"While Villiers gets away?"

"He will not be within a hundred klicks of here," added Beyett.

"And that is a reason stop, lay down, and do nothing?"

"Nobody is doing nothing," snapped Corwin, "A whole army is right around the corner, and would be all too happy to blow holes in us. Let's not give them that opportunity."

"Army of normals. We are better than that."

"Individually, yes," replied Beyett.

"But you'd be a fool to think we can take on armies by ourselves," said Corwin.

Nylund sighed and turned around to address the rest of them.

"Is this what you want to do? Sit around and wait?"

No one replied.

"Well, I am not one for waiting."

"Sit down!" ordered Corwin.

But Nylund continued.

"The Sergeant may have got us into this mess, but if he's not willing or able to get us out, then maybe it's time someone else did."

"He's still the boss."

"No...he isn't, Vi. That life is gone. Our army, our support, our everything. It's just us now, twelve idiots with no home, no side, no nothing. Our ranks, our history; none of it counts for shit. I say we get out there and start getting some intel and bust some heads."

Corwin reached forward and kicked Nylund's legs out from under him. He landed hard on the relatively dry dirt ground. Corwin moved to put a boot onto his chest, but Nylund rolled out the way and jumped nimbly back onto his feet and into a fighting stance.

"I'm still in charge here, so don't you forget it," growled Corwin.

"I say you aren't."

"Come on, enough of this." Beyett stepped up to intervene, but nobody else did.

Porter smiled, as he lay with his back against a tree, just waiting for the blows to start. Hunter was frozen in disbelief and could not find the words to say or make his body move to interfere. Corwin pushed Beyett back.

"No, this has been brewing, so let's get it out here and now. Nylund, you're a cocky son of a bitch who could have led this squad if you'd had the fucking balls to step up and be a man. At least now you've manned up enough to speak your mind."

"All right, Corwin, lets settle this."

He pulled his rifle strap over his head, placing the weapon against the nearest tree, and then took up his fighting stance once again. Corwin approached confidently with his hands held low.

"Ain't nobody gonna stop this?"

"Why should we, Beyett?" Rane asked.

"Not like there is anything else to keep us entertained," added Vi.

Nylund made a quick jab towards Corwin's face, but he voided it and returned an even quicker straight punch of his own. Nylund seemed stunned by the speed, and Corwin's body language was of a man that had already won the fight before it had even begun. Nylund kicked for his leg, but Corwin casually moved it back and went right back at him with a single punch. It struck him square in the face and launched him back until he rocked to a halt, his back impacting with a tree.

"If you want this so bad. If you really want it, then prove it. Your half-hearted attempts at taking over this team are pathetic. Win or lose this; it's time you stepped up, and manned up to be the soldier we all need you to be."

That infuriated Nylund and he came rushing at Corwin with a new found sense of anger and determination. He struck forward with two quick jabs and then leapt with a flying knee, though it did not get high enough to strike Corwin's face, and was instead brushed aside by his body armour.

Corwin locked his arms around Nylund's head, turned and threw him over his back so that he landed face first in the dirt. But he quickly leapt forward and rushed low at Corwin and got a firm grapple around his waist. He lifted him off the ground and carried on until he was smashed hard against a tree. Corwin drove an elbow down onto Nylund's collar, and it was enough shock and pain to release his hold. Corwin shoved him back and delivered a powerful kick into the centre of his body.

The power of the blow caused Nylund to fly back two metres, hitting the ground on his back and sliding to a halt in the dirt. He was in pain but tried to get up, only to find Lecia's foot stamping down on his chest and pinning him to the ground.

"Enough," she said.

Nylund tried to struggle for just a moment, but Lecia raised her hand to reveal her pistol in hand and aimed it right at his face. He stopped in shock and looked into her eyes to see she wasn't fooling around, and he nodded in agreement. She took her foot off and casually walked away as he got up, trying to find some shred of dignity as they all looked at him with a mixture of anger and disappointment. Only Porter was still grinning like an idiot; his sadistic sense of humour only wanted to see more of Nylund's suffering.

"Don't pity or hate him," said Corwin, "Confidence, pride, ambition, I want it all in each and every one of you. The job lying before us requires nothing less than everything we can be. If you think you can do my job better than I do it, then do something about it, you got that?"

There was agreement, but nobody actually said a word.

"Tonight all hell is going to break loose. Beyett says the operation here was a disaster, but it also should have happened a year ago, so we just don't know what to expect. Either way, there will be a level of panic and mayhem that should allow us to move a little more easily."

"And where will we go?" asked Vi.

Corwin stopped a moment; he hadn't fully worked that out for himself.

"If Beyett is right, then Villiers is working with the Germans, and he must be pretty high up to have implemented such changes. First thing, we find some Germans and beat the facts out of them."

"Porter smiled, and Rane, too, but Tano looked less than impressed.

"Great plan," he added.

"If you can think of a better one, then I'm all ears."

"If you want to stand any chance of getting to Villiers, and he is as big a deal to the Germans as you think he is, and I think you're probably right, you won't be able to get to him by force. You can't get through the whole German army by yourself."

"We can try," Rane joined in.

"Come on, be realistic. If we are going to get to Villiers, we must infiltrate the German forces."

"Infiltrate?" asked Corwin, "We are soldiers, not spies. We don't know the first thing about infiltration. We have no knowledge or back-story to work with. We don't look or sound remotely the part for it. We don't even speak German!"

"I do," he replied with a confident grin.

"When the fuck did you learn that?" asked Vi.

"Probably when you were whoring around," said Harland.

She looked at him in disgust to see there was no humour

in his face at all. He genuinely hated her for what she was, and she him for his attitude, but Tano went on.

"I watch, I read, I learn, and I understand far more than you ever can begin to imagine."

Corwin was looking to Beyett for an opinion, and he simply shrugged.

"Okay, so one among us could get away with this, what about the rest of us, Tano?"

"Get us the uniforms, a couple of vehicles, and enough gear to look the part, and I will handle it."

"Like all the stuff we left at that house?" Vi asked him.

"Riddled with holes and stained with blood, not quite the impression that will sell this."

Corwin was glad to hear some plan was coming together.

"All right, in the confusion of the impending attack we should be able to make this work. We wait for the cover of night, and then we'll see if we can find what we're looking for. But we do nothing until the fighting starts. We start things too early and we could damage the Allies' mission, and risk being hunted down before all this has kicked off. This is all on the fly right now, and I am aware of that. I wish I could tell you we had more intel, a better plan, and teams of analysts working to help us out, but we don't. All we have is each other, and that is what we must rely on."

He went back to his former position and sat down to take it easy, knowing there was nothing more they could do. Beyett pulled something out of his pocket. It was paper and folded many times over. He opened it out to reveal a map of France. It looked as though it was already twenty years old and was a little fragile. Beyett pointed to where they were, and Corwin ran his hand over the paper until he found the border of Germany.

"We aren't even that far away."

"That's no distance at all in the life we came from, but with wheeled vehicles, and the quantity of soldiers between us and there, it'll feel a whole lot longer than you think."

"If you were Villiers, where would you be?"

Beyett shook his head.

"Somewhere deep in the heart of Germany. Somewhere far from the risk of attack from the air, and where he can work, develop, and scheme. Perhaps even right by Hitler's side."

"You think he could have wormed his way into government that easily?"

"You know what Hitler was always obsessed with? Among other things."

Corwin shook his head.

"Wonder weapons. Villiers could have promised him the Earth, and actually delivered on that. I've no doubt he will be up there at the top."

Corwin shook his head. "We were so close. I had him in my sights, so close to ending it all, and now this. Everything we ever worked for has counted for nothing."

"No, not nothing," replied Beyett, "All that work has led to us. We are the sole creations and endeavours of the civilised and free world. It is a massive burden to endure, but it is ours to carry."

CHAPTER FIVE

The sun was finally going down, and they were all restless and waiting for some sign of the beginnings of an operation. None of them was used to having to lie in wait for anything. Hunter couldn't help but stare at Frasi. The man appeared little older than him, but they were nothing alike. He wanted to follow in Corwin's footsteps with all his heart, and he couldn't see how anyone else wouldn't. Frasi sat on the perimeter of them all, out of talking distance from the rest. Though everyone knew that with his hearing he probably heard everything they said.

He was alert and on watch all the time. He came across as feral in many ways, barely speaking or interacting with them in any way, and yet his loyalty appeared unflinching. Hunter couldn't resist going over to talk to him and try and glean some sense of his character from him. Frasi didn't turn to look at him, but it was clear he was aware of his approach in his peripheral vision. Hunter knelt down beside him and hoped for some words to come, but they didn't, not from Frasi.

"You don't like people all that much, do you?"

"I don't hate people. I just feel better when they aren't around," he replied sternly.

Hunter was taken aback by the comment and took it as his cue to retreat back to Corwin, who was smiling. He had not heard the words, but could already see in Hunter's face he had been sent packing.

"Not the most talkative of people, is he?" Hunter asked, sitting down beside Corwin.

Corwin's smile dissipated as he explained.

"We found Frasi in some wasteland of a city. There was just nothing left, nothing but him. I don't know how he survived or how long he had been there. He will never say, and I'll never push him."

Hunter's face turned to stone, realising how inappropriate he had been.

"But he's one of us? An ape?"

"Who knows what he is? He's certainly got enhanced abilities from somewhere. When he found us, he tried to steal from us. Just food, and almost got away with it, till Lecia put a shot through him at two hundred metres. We didn't know who or what he was, but clearly he didn't mean us harm. We patched him up and gave him a few days' rations and went on our way, but he tagged along with us. Stowed away in a box on the back of my DART. Crazy son of a bitch rode in that box for hours. He's not left our side since."

"So he's not even officially part of the Regiment?"

"Officially?" Corwin smiled, "Nobody is gonna stir up trouble for a man who chooses to go fight and do everything he can for those around him. Anyway, none of that matters now. We're all strangers lost in a foreign world together. Maybe knowing we all share that same feeling will bring him some peace."

Corwin instinctively looked down at the pad on his arm once more as he had so many times recently. He wanted some news, some information, but there was nothing. He felt completely blind and deaf to the world without the technology they so heavily relied on. Then, just as he hoped for some sign, they heard explosions erupt in the distance. At first just a few, and then their frequency increased to such volume it was just a constant drone as the areas around them were carpet-bombed.

"This is it. This is the beginning," said Beyett.

"Can we finally go kill something?"

Corwin shook his head at Porter.

"Not yet, this is just the start."

"How long do we wait?"

"One hour."

Beyett agreed with him. "That should give some time for the Allied forces to arrive, but a long way before seaborne landings."

"How else are they getting here?" asked Hunter.

Corwin pointed up to the sky.

"Parachute and glider."

Hunter seemed amazed. The concepts weren't entirely alien to him, but he'd never seen either with his own eyes. When the bombing finally came to a close, it was soon followed by the thunder of ship guns joining the assault. The time passed quicker now, and all were eager to go when Corwin finally got up to move.

"Stay quiet, stay safe. Don't fire unless absolutely necessary. Don't reveal yourselves to anyone, and never kill an Allied soldier."

"Even if they would try and kill us?"

Corwin knew it was hard to accept.

"We have no friends in this world, Vi, so let's try and make some, okay? You encounter any Allied forces, then you do everything in your power to ensure they don't get hurt."

"And if we encounter these Allies, and for some reason they don't try and shoot us, but want to know who the hell we are?" Nylund asked.

"Beyett, got any ideas?"

"We can try and blend in as part of them."

"Think that will work?"

Beyett shook his head. "I doubt it."

"Then we are a Ranger unit."

"And people will buy that?" asked Vi.

Corwin shrugged. "It's worth a shot. Come on, let's move out."

He led them back to the track they came in on and then southeast, away from where the main offensive would likely come. As they reached the edge of the tree line, Corwin heard the sound of engines. He raised his hand quickly, calling them to a halt and to duck down in the foliage. Their multi-terrain camouflage worked relatively well, especially since most of the desert dust and sand had been washed away by their unexpected plunge into the lake the day before. He gestured for Beyett to come up beside him. The genius among them had never been so close to his side in a warzone before, but Corwin increasingly had to rely on his knowledge of history.

Three small tanks rode into view. They looked lightweight and lightly armoured, carried four drive wheels without any bogeys, and a stubby barrelled gun in a small turret.

"German?"

Beyett shook his head at Corwin. They could finally make out the Allied star painted over the front of the hull as they tore past them at quite a speed.

"How the fuck did they get here so soon?"

"I don't remember what they're called, but I recall the Allies flying light tanks in with gliders at times in this war."

"A tank in a glider? Who the fuck would be crazy enough to do that?"

"Desperate times call for desperate measures, Vi, and you work with what you have," replied Beyett.

"They gonna do any good?" asked Corwin.

Beyett shook his head. "Who knows? But if they are here, that must mean there have been substantial airborne landings. We must be careful."

Corwin got up and led them across the open field and beyond. They reached the outskirts of a small town. There were no lights on for fear of bombings. This made their work all the more easy. Most windows were covered up with shutters as the civilians hunkered down in hope of survival. Corwin stopped them once more when he saw a glimmer of movement. A German soldier walked out of the front door of a house. His rifle was slung over his shoulder as he lit up a cigarette. Corwin looked to Frasi and simply nodded.

They stayed put and watched Frasi run to the back of the house without making a sound. A few seconds later he appeared behind the soldier and drew a knife across his throat before he even noticed he wasn't alone. Frasi took the weight of the man as he fell and dragged him quietly back into a bush the other side of the house.

Engines roared once again, and they dashed to the side of the same house. Five trucks full of soldiers rushed past on the road to Dieppe. They were running with blackout lights only and were completely loaded with troops.

"Whole lot of uniforms we could have used there," said Vi.

"Like you'll be wearing them."

She looked confused by Porter's sentiment.

"You know what the Nazis thought of women?"

She shook her head.

"Only good for fucking and making babies."

She spat on the ground beside him in disgust.

"Maybe they had a point," he added, just to piss her off.

"He's an asshole, but he's still right," Lecia said, passing them by. Corwin signalled for them to be quiet; they could hear vehicles heading their way once again, but this time from the west towards a small crossroads up ahead.

"Sure is getting a little busy round here," whispered Beyett.

They waited and watched, and a car came into view. It was a large and luxurious four-door officers' command car. There were recognition markings fluttering in the wind from the wings, but it meant nothing to any of them.

"Got to be someone important?"

Beyett nodded to Corwin. A truck followed close behind, and as soon as they had gone past the junction, Corwin signalled for them to go forward. He rushed across the road and into the garden of the house opposite, leaping clean over a fence. They went from one garden to another, running in parallel with the convoy and almost able to keep up, for they were travelling at a relaxed pace. They covered almost half a klick like that when Corwin stopped them. He'd seen the vehicles pull up to the lavish gates of a manor house and stop in the front courtyard.

There were two guards posted at the gate, and they could see huge red banners with swastikas hanging from the columns on the front of the structure.

"Aiming a little high, aren't we?" Beyett was looking at the grandeur of the mansion.

"Isn't that the way we always roll?"

Beyett couldn't disagree, but he didn't like it. They watched carefully as a soldier opened the door of the car, and two officers stepped out. Both wore lavishly decorated uniforms, clearly high-ranking officials.

"Struck gold," said Porter.

Corwin watched as every soldier they passed avoided eye contact and simply saluted without hesitation.

"We get that car and those uniforms, we could get far," said Tano.

"I'll get them for you," Rane said in his usual gruff voice.

Corwin smiled.

"I think this one might need a bit more of a delicate touch than you have to offer."

"Come on, let me at 'em."

"We aren't even going to be able to fit you in one of those uniforms," Tano said, looking at the hulking figure of Rane.

"He's got a point," replied Corwin, "Look at us, trying to blend in to this world. It's a fucking disaster."

"No, it might just work yet."

"Think we should choose a slightly less ambitious target?"

"No, Nylund, time isn't on our side, and this will do us

just fine."

Corwin looked carefully at the whole building and everything around it. A two-metre high iron fence ran for several hundred metres in either direction until it met a small wood on either side. There was little cover, but it was so dark the flat ground leading up to the structure was almost completely obscured.

"Here's the deal. Rane, Nylund, you're taking the two on the gate. Lecia, find some high ground where you can cover the frontage of the building, and you fire the moment those two make their move. Beyett, you stick with Lecia. We cannot afford you risking your life. We need you more than ever. Hunter, Chas, and Vi, you're with me taking the left hand side. Tano, Frasi, Harland, take the left flank."

He stopped and looked at Porter, and just knew he could be a spanner in the works.

"What?" Porter asked, smiling.

"Don't fuck this up for us," said Corwin.

Porter shrugged while he still smiled.

"All right, you're with me, too," he said, knowing he needed to keep an eye on the ruthless and erratic soldier.

"Nobody fires a weapon save for Lecia unless you absolutely have to. We work through this place silent and smooth, and leave none alive. We do not let any signal get out. We do not damage those vehicles or wreck the uniforms of the brass we just saw go inside. I cannot stress that enough. You all with me on this?"

They all nodded agreement, and he slung his captured rifle onto his back, hoping to not need it. He looked to Rane and Porter one last time and prayed they could approach the situation with the stealth and caution that was required; he'd never seen evidence of that from either before. He sighed, realising how unlikely it was to work before heading onwards.

"Bet you can't wait to slip into one of those snazzy uniforms?" Porter joked to Corwin as they made their way quietly through foliage to reach the far edge of the fence where they could get over without being noticed.

"You know I wonder how in the hell you ever stay fighting on our side. You'd fit right in with the enemy with how fucked up your thoughts are."

Porter shrugged and seemed mildly curious.

"But I'm one of the good guys, aren't I?"

"That remains to be seen. It's never too late to disappoint."

"Now you're getting it."

"What?"

"That life really is as fucked up as I see it. It's all a joke."

"A joke you keep living?"

"What else is there to do but hang on and enjoy the ride?"

It was clear from the look in his eyes he wasn't joking. He was the only one amongst them who was genuinely enjoying himself. They reached the edge of the railings and passed through a gap in the trees nearby and found themselves at the edge of the open field alongside the manner house. Corwin stopped for just a moment to look around. He went to step out when he felt Porter's hand grab his shoulder and haul him back into cover. He was about to protest when he noticed Porter's other hand over his shoulder and pointed out to their left flank.

In the shadows, he could just make out a tiny glimmer of movement and squinted to make out the shape of a guard slowly ambling along the tree line.

"Just wait," whispered Porter.

A few seconds later they saw the silhouette of Chas leaping out from the trees next to the soldier and land on his shoulders, with her legs wrapped around his waist. She gripped his head with both hands, and in one motion snapped his neck. He'd had no time to even think about defending himself.

"Beautiful, isn't it?" Porter asked, as they watched the man collapse. Chas landed numbly on her feet over her victim, "To watch such a figure deal death without a worry in the world. It's art, and it's beautiful."

Corwin shook his head.

"You never cease to amaze me. We're facing a crisis the likes we have never known, that the world has never known, and you're obsessing over tits and ass?"

Porter shrugged; he had no shame at all.

"You've fucked her, and you think the same. You're just too hung up on some sense of morality and pride to admit what I am willing to. Who's fucked up now?"

He couldn't deny it. For all of Porter's negative qualities, he never lied, and he always said it how he saw it, however twisted that might be. It made Corwin stop and think before remembering he had work to do.

"Don't fuck this up for us now," he said to Porter.

But he only smiled in response with his typical nihilistic sense of humour. Corwin drew out his knife and hunched low as he began moving across the open ground. He could feel his pulse rising as they drew nearer. They could just see the silhouette of the house, but there was so little moonlight they could make out no detail at all. Then as they got to fifteen metres from the perimeter, Corwin stopped on seeing the faintest of lights glow in front of him. He froze and watched the light grow a little brighter from a cigarette in a soldier's mouth as he drew back on it.

Corwin flipped the knife, caught it by the blade, and launched it with speed and precision. The tip penetrated the soldier's right eye and drove through his skull, the hilt stopping dead at the eye socket. He rushed forwards and caught the body before it crashed to the stone wall running around the house. He let the body down carefully, drawing out the blade and wiping the blood off on the uniform of the dead German beneath him.

The dead soldier didn't wear the armour he had seen on those the previous day, and carried a rifle far more antiquated than the assault rifle Corwin had taken. It was exactly as he expected a soldier of the Third Reich to look, and that was some relief; things hadn't changed too drastically, or he hoped so, anyway.

He moved along the wall to double doors leading into the house. Above them was a window open on the first floor. He looked to Chas and pointed up. She took a run at the wall and jumped, landing with her hands on the frame of the window, nimbly pulling herself inside without a sound. Corwin reached for the handle of the door and slowly turned it as to not make a sound. He smiled on finding no resistance; it was unlocked. He pulled the door open and stepped inside to some kind of washroom. It was in darkness, although he could just see some light creeping inside from candles in the next room.

Porter, Hunter, and Vi followed him in. He looked down at his knife and suddenly felt incredibly vulnerable, as if he'd entered the lion's den unprepared. He drew his pistol with his left hand and carried onwards to the light, stopping when he noticed a soldier sitting at a typewriter in the hallway next to a broad staircase. He was facing the front door of the house. Through a glass pane Corwin could see one of the guards standing at the entrance.

He watched and waited until he saw the guard drop lifelessly to the ground. The man looked up in shock on seeing the movement out of the corner of his eye and got up to investigate, but Corwin took his opening. He leapt forward and wrapped his arm around the man's neck in a chokehold so that he could not make a sound and gripped tightly. The terrified soldier resisted for just a few seconds before passing out. Porter reached the typewriter and stared at it with an odd sense of curiosity, then turned his attention to a plate of cheese beside the machine. He picked up one of the blocks and took a bite, picked up the cheese wire next to it, and smiled.

Corwin pointed for Vi and Hunter to take the ground floor; he and Porter took the stairs to the next level. They crept slowly and cautiously. Corwin winced as so many of the wooden slats creaked under foot. As they got half way up, they were relieved to hear music. It was sung in French and meant nothing to them. They reached the top of the stairs; the music was coming from a room along the hall. They crept closer, and Corwin peered around the corner.

Inside were twelve soldiers lying around playing cards and drinking wine. It was if they had not a care in the world. Corwin tried to understand how they could go on so casually with the Allied operation having begun. Maybe they didn't know about it, which seemed preposterous considering the bombardment, or they simply weren't threatened by it. Either way, it was unsettling. He noticed one of the men get up and say a few words before heading for the door. He ducked back out of the way and signalled the danger to Porter. They waited either side of the door for the man to exit. As he did so, he stopped and turned in shock to see Corwin. Before he could get a word out, Porter threw the cheese wire over the soldier's head and pulled down tight.

The wire cut into the man's flesh and suffocated him enough that there was no sound at all. Porter held on tight and dragged him back well out of view. As the man went limp, he lifted him up like a ragdoll and placed him in a nearby room that was quiet and dark. Corwin paced up to him and whispered into his ear.

"Wait here. I'm going up. Do not engage them unless you absolutely have to."

Porter nodded, but he wasn't sure how much he believed he would follow the order. Corwin carried on to the next flight of stairs, and once again carefully ascended them. As he reached the top, he found the body of a soldier with no marks at all, and knew it was Chas' work. He spotted her looking through the keyhole of a large pair of double doors. Corwin stepped up to her slowly and looked himself. He could see two officers sitting with their feet up on a large office table and smoking cigarillos. A gramophone blasted out the same track he had heard before.

"We need those uniforms. There can be no blood," he whispered to Chas, "How can we do this?"

She smiled in response and took two paces back. She unzipped and stepped out of her boots, slipped her combat trousers off, pulling off the skin-tight jacket and body armour she sported in one. She wore intricately woven white lace underwear. He smiled at the prospect of her going into battle that way, but it didn't surprise him.

She pulled out the tie in her hair and let her long curly blond hair flow out onto her shoulders. Corwin couldn't believe the transformation. She looked like she could be a vintage pin-up girl.

She waved him back to get out of the way, stepped up to the doorway, and knocked the door gently three times.

"Hereinkommen!" a voice yelled brashly from inside.

She smiled at Corwin briefly, and he could see a sexy, but wickedly devious glint in her eye. She turned back and swung the two doors open slowly before pushing out her hips, placing one hand on her hip and the other to her lips. Corwin couldn't help but smile as he looked at her beautiful body shining in the candlelight.

He could hear the leers of the two Germans inside saying something he didn't understand, and she strode into the room. He peered around the corner to watch her go to work. They were so intoxicated by her they didn't even notice him watching it all unfold.

She stepped up to the desk and leaned over to rest her elbows on the top. One of the officers got up and just marvelled at her before smacking her ass. She looked around and smiled in response, but Corwin could tell her enjoyment was coming from something very different than what they were expecting. He pulled his hand back to spank her once again, but as his hand rose up, she spun around and hit the man's throat with a knife hand strike. His windpipe was crushed, and he collapsed unable to breathe.

The other man jumped to his feet and reached for the pistol at his side, but she jumped over the table and launched her feet high over his body, wrapping them around his throat. He staggered back against the wall behind his desk and reached up to try to stop her chokehold. But she arched upwards and held on firm, punching him in the temple with three hard and precise strikes. He was stunned, and she only squeezed harder between her legs until he passed out. The two of them slumped down behind the desk beyond Corwin's view.

He stepped into the room as she arose from the desk with a bizarre smile on her face. She looked like a women who'd just won a beauty pageant. Her joy looked so innocent, and he could only shake his head in amazement.

"You're a fucking psycho, you know that, right?"

She smiled and licked her lips, running her hands over her body in a blatant show off before him.

"Grab your gear. Our work is far from done."

"Yes, Boss," she replied.

"Start stripping their uniforms. I have something to take care of downstairs."

He continued on down the stairway to where Porter was awaiting him, nodding to him as he approached, and they both knew it was time. Porter pulled out a German stick grenade he had liberated and twisted the priming cap off.

"No, wait," said Corwin, but his whispers were too quiet to be heard.

The reckless Porter tossed it into the room before he could even get into position. They heard a spate of cries and panicked shouts from those in the room before the explosion rang out, and could hear glass shattering on the ground outside as the windows were blown out.

"You crazy son of a bitch!" Corwin yelled.

But Porter ignored him and stepped into the doorway of the room. His rifle was held at the hip, and he opened up on full auto, cutting down the survivors as they desperately reached for any weapon to hand. Corwin couldn't even get in as he blocked the only entrance, and Porter didn't release his finger from the trigger until the magazine ran empty.

Finally, as all went silent, he went into the room and up to the last soldier still moving, clubbing his skull with the butt of his rifle until he stopped moving. Corwin stepped inside to see it was utter carnage, only to find Porter kneeling down beside one of his victims. But he wasn't doing so out of any remorse or concern. He pulled out the metal tin of cigarillos from the dead soldier's tunic pocket and proceeded to light one up.

"Was that really necessary?"

"Think of a better way of taking out a room full of guys? Not like we could have done it quiet," he replied, smoking the cigarillo and breathing out a puff of smoke with a triumphant smirk.

Corwin went to the top of the stairs and yelled, "Everyone okay?"

"All clear!" Vi answered.

"Could be a nice spot to rest out the night," said Porter.

"Really? A Nazi HQ when the Allied invasion has already begun? We want to be as far away from here as we possibly can. Let's round up everything we need and get the hell out of here."

Rane, Nylund, Vi, and Hunter appeared at the base of the stairs and awaited his orders.

"Take everything you can get. Find the best uniforms you can, and load up those vehicles with all the ammo there is. Fifteen minutes and we are out of here."

They separated to do as ordered. He rushed back

upstairs to find Tano already dressing himself in one of the officer's uniforms, while Chas was still in her underwear and stripping the other body. She took off the last item and then proceeded towards him to present the mound of clothing.

"What do I want with this?" Corwin asked.

"You have to be the other officer in this," replied Tano.

"Why?"

"Because you are in charge. Don't worry, I will do any talking that needs to be done."

Corwin took the uniform. His knowledge of history wasn't great, but he knew how awful the Nazi regime was, and he looked at the uniform with disgust.

"Whatever it takes, remember," said Tano to reassure him, "All the horrible things you've had to do, and you are balking at having to wear an offensive uniform?"

"Sergeant, we've got incoming!" Nylund shouted.

"He rushed to the edge of the stairs.

"Who and how many?"

"No idea, but they're coming in fast!"

"Take up positions. Cover all entry points, and keep your heads down!"

CHAPTER SIX

Corwin rushed to the window in the room where Porter had thrown the grenade. He dragged one of the bodies away from the blown window and stood beside it, peering out just enough to get a look at what was coming their way. He knew Lecia was still out there with Beyett. That gave him some relief, and also a fear of what might become of them.

You see them?" he asked Porter who was at the next window.

"No."

But even as he spoke, they saw movement in front of the gates. At first it was just a few men, and then more and more, until they could see a whole platoon forming there, and at least another platoon moving off to each flank. He could already tell they were not Germans. Their equipment was completely different, and he noticed a number wore red berets. He knew that as the iconic symbol of the British airborne.

"Run or fight?"

Corwin didn't know how to answer.

"They're the good guys. We can't fight them, and we won't make it out on foot."

"We have to do something."

Corwin knew it was the case, but he had no idea what to do. He rushed back to the stairs.

"These are the good guys. Do not fire on them! I repeat, do not fire on them!" he yelled for all to hear, but he wasn't sure they would follow the order.

The platoon at the entrance passed through the open gates and rushed towards the front of the manor house, ducking down behind two parked vehicles for cover. Corwin shook his head; he had fought so hard to protect their new method of transport, and here they were slap bang in the middle of a potential gun battle.

They waited and watched, as the British soldiers seemed to wait and assess what they were seeing. The bodies of the German guards still lay scattered about the site, and that clearly made them both curious and suspicious.

"Identify yourselves!" a voice finally yelled in a deep and crisply spoken English accent.

"Sergeant Corwin, Rangers!"

He knew it was a vague response, but he just had to hope they could get away with it. There was silence for a moment.

"What is the code word?"

Shit! He knew they were in trouble.

"We've been operating here for three months and have not had comms for some time. We are a covert outfit! We knew this operation was happening, but have not been party to the specifics!"

He knew he was making stuff up and trying to bullshit

his way through now, but it was all he could think.

"Show yourself!"

What the hell!

"Don't do it. They'll take a shot at you," said Porter.

"We have to try."

"Why?"

"Because the only other option is to fight, and I will not have their blood on our hands."

"But you'd be happy with your own?"

He shook his head and slowly stepped out into the opening. It was a low window, so he was visible from the knees upwards. One of the soldiers stepped up from behind the staff car and walked forward to get a better view.

"Sergeant, I am unaware of any Rangers operating in this area in the passing weeks or today. Care to provide some more proof of your identity."

"Is it not enough that you can see what we have achieved here?"

The man shook his head.

"My name is Captain Reeves, and my mission was to capture key German officers at this location. Can you explain what the hell you are doing here?"

"I told you, Captain. We have been operating as clandestine forces and saw this opportunity, so we took it."

The Captain squinted as he tried to get a better view of Corwin. He could see the armour and camouflage he was wearing, and it was obvious he was becoming suspicious.

"Sergeant, without confirmation of who you are, I must ask that you lay your your arms and come out peacefully. If you are who you say you are, and it can be confirmed, then all is well."

"And if we refuse?"

"Sergeant, if you refuse, then I must assume that you are the enemy, and you will be fired upon."

"Fuck this. If they are in our way, we put them down," said Porter.

"No," snapped Corwin, "You will not fire on these men."

"Sergeant, lay down your weapons and step outside. You have thirty seconds to comply!"

Corwin sighed, trying to work out some way out of their situation.

"Twenty seconds, Sergeant!"

The time seemed to fly by.

"Ten seconds!"

"Five…four…three…two…one! Last chance, Sergeant!"

"You don't have to do this. You don't want this!" Corwin shouted.

"Time is up. Come out without your weapons!"

But he shook his head. The Captain went back to the cover of the car. Corwin stepped away from the window and to the top of the stairs where everyone could hear him.

"Nobody uses lethal force! Nobody! You kill one of them, and I'll kill you!" he barked.

The first stick rushed for the door, and Corwin heard a racket as Rane and Nylund engaged them in hand-to-hand in the darkness of the hallway.

"Ah, fuck it," Corwin murmured.

He put down his rifle and took a run at the opening where there was once a window and jumped. He cleared the car in what was a superhuman jump and landed in amongst the Captain and his stick. They were all too shocked to respond initially, due to the amazing stunt he had achieved, and the inability to fire for he was in amongst them.

He reached for the first shoulder, drove a knee hard into his stomach, and knocked him out with a punch to the head. He back-fisted another and then drove a kick into the third. The power of the blow launched the man into the air in a display of power none of them had seen before.

Gunshots rang out from one of them firing point blank with a submachine gun at Corwin. The armour on his torso was riddled with bullets, but not one of them went through. The shocked gunman stopped. Corwin grabbed him and launched him through the air. He turned to take on another when he felt the cold metal of a gun muzzle against the side of his head.

He froze. He knew that no matter how strong he was, no matter how fast he healed, he could not survive a bullet to the head like that. His eyes panned over slightly to see it was the Captain himself holding a revolver.

"What are you?"

"Sergeant Corwin," he replied confidently.

"Of where? Your story does not add up, Sergeant. Tell your men to lay down their arms and come out without a fight, and I promise you no harm will come to you."

He waited for a response, and Corwin knew he had to agree.

"Come on out!" he boomed at the top of his voice, "It's over! Come out and put your weapons down!"

The Captain was still racking his brains trying to make

sense of it.

"You lied about who you are, and yet you took down this whole place, why?"

"Some truths you don't want to know, Captain. All you need to know is that we are not your enemy, not even close."

"I wish I could believe that. I really do."

"Then do. Some truths are stranger than fiction."

"And you believe that, as a military man? Clearly, you are no German, but I don't know what you are."

They turned and watched the rest of Corwin's squad step out from the house under the watchful eyes of dozens of airborne soldiers. Several balked at the sight of the mountain of a man that Rane was. He was freakishly huge, to a degree that none of them could believe he was just human, and they would be right. But it was as the three women came out they were most shocked.

"Those three are with you?" Reeves asked in astonishment, "Not a single element of the United States armed forces would allow women in a combat role."

"Times change, Captain."

It wasn't a lie, and he didn't know how else to explain it. The British soldiers were studying every element of their equipment and trying to understand what they were seeing.

"Who the hell are you people?" Reeves asked, signalling for his people to take their weapons off them.

"We are a specialist unit that uses only the latest in technologies and tactics. We are an unorthodox unit granted, but I can guarantee you, we are not your enemy."

He could see the Captain wanted to believe him, and their lack of use of lethal force reinforced that fact.

"I am sorry, Sergeant, but we have to work on facts, known facts. Maybe you are with us, but you've offered no proof or explanation to support that. I will, however, ensure that no harm comes to you. You will be shipped back where your story can be confirmed."

Corwin nodded in acceptance, although it was far from the response he was hoping for.

"Until such time as what you say can be proven, you will be considered enemy combatants, and you must comply with our orders. No harm will come to you unless you resist."

Corwin nodded and looked over to his team, hoping they would accept the ruling.

Reeves turned to one of his people.

"Get that truck going. We're getting this lot back to the boats."

"Yes, Sir," the response came.

He turned back to Corwin. "There were two high-ranking German officers at this manor. Do you know of their whereabouts?"

"Both dead."

"Your doing?"

Corwin nodded.

"You took his house without a single casualty?" he asked suspiciously.

"It's what we do, and we're the best," replied Corwin confidently.

The truck engine started, and Reeves ushered them all aboard, along with a stick of his own platoon. As they began to pull away, they could see the soldiers carrying out the bodies of the two German officers for identification. Both were stripped to their underwear and bore no physical marks of injury. Reeves looked back to Corwin as they rode away. There were a hundred questions in his eyes, and yet Corwin knew there was no way he could have answered any of them honestly.

They rode on for just a hundred metres when Porter leaned across to whisper to Corwin.

"So when we getting out of this?"

"We're not."

Several others of the team heard the conversation and looked to him with amazement.

"We can't go on like this. Trying to hide from both sides in a war that encompasses the world. If we hope to have any chance of success, we need help."

"And you think we're gonna get help here? What we're gonna get is a prison cell," replied Porter.

"The Sergeant is right," added Beyett, "Alone we stand no chance of ever reaching Villiers. As a unit we are strong, stronger than a hundred ordinary men, or more. But without the intelligence, support, and technology that made us what we are, we are worth little more than any other squad."

Porter laughed. "Keep dreaming."

But nobody else found it funny. They passed several platoons of British infantry on the road heading northwest to the beaches. They could hear bombers passing overhead, and always the sound of artillery firing on both sides.

"You said this operation was a disaster?" Hunter asked Beyett.

"It was, but it went nothing like this. They never got off the beaches, and they never used airborne forces. Whatever has changed in this timeline, the war will progress in a very different fashion to the history I know."

"Great, so we've lost that advantage, too," replied Nylund.

"No, it's all useful information. Sure some things have changed, but plenty will have remained the same," Corwin replied in some attempt to calm them down.

"Gonna be an awful lot of questions when they get us back to England," said Beyett.

"Questions we don't have the right answers for. Should have just fought our way out and gone on with the mission."

"No, Porter, enough lies."

They looked at Corwin as he went on.

"They won't work. We can't bullshit our way through this. We couldn't even convince once field officer that our story was solid, so how do you think that will work when we have some serious interrogators before us? No, from now on, transparency. They aren't willing to believe the bullshit, fine, let's hit them with the truth."

"What are you saying?"

"That we state the facts, Beyett. Who we are, where we came from, and why we're here."

"That's madness. We'll be locked up, and they'll throw away the keys. You know how crazy this all sounds if you aren't the ones to experience it? Would you have ever believed a story if some strangers turned up in our time with this tale?"

Corwin shook his head.

"No, but we have truth on our side."

Porter laughed.

"Truth, you think people want the truth?" He laughed once again.

"I don't see we have any other choice left. We have

some proof. We have technology that is far beyond this age."

"That is all dead," replied Beyett.

"We have powers and strengths that are superhuman."

"If anything, they'll probably believe we are some kind of Nazi experiment. It's about the most likely answer. Especially as you can damn well guarantee Villiers has been implementing his ideas for enhanced soldiers by now. We'll be seen as freaks and creations of the enemy," said Beyett.

"Got any better idea?" Corwin asked coldly, resting back against the bench seat of the truck.

They could all see he was calm and completely serious, and none of them had a better solution.

"Exactly. We go along with this and don't cause trouble. We prove we aren't the enemy and that we can be trusted, and we can gain the support we need."

Beyett shook his head, and yet he could find no other solution. They reached the beaches and saw hundreds of ships and smaller boats out at sea, as well as endless lines of landing craft, tanks, and trucks on the beaches.

"This is not how it went at all."

They all waited for him to go on as the truck rocked to a halt on the beach.

"This is like some hybrid between the disaster of Dieppe, and the triumphant success and logistical marvel of D-day, all rolled into one."

"And which do you think it will be, disaster or triumph?" asked Corwin.

Beyett shook his head.

"I just don't know, anymore."

As their truck came to a halt on the shoreline, Porter

made one last attempt to convince Corwin to change his mind.

"Last chance, we can fight our way out of this now, or be caged for God knows how long."

Corwin glared at him.

"Don't you dare try and fuck this up. We stick to plan. Transparency and honesty, it's the only hope we have left."

They were ushered off the truck and towards the beach, wading up to their knees before clambering aboard a rickety open top landing craft. The ramp slammed home before them. Corwin could see the look of absolute loss and defeat in the eyes of them all, except for Beyett.

"It was the right thing to do," he said to reassure Corwin who was not entirely convinced.

They soon found themselves aboard a small warship and heading for England. It was a bizarre turn of events, but Corwin started to feel some relief that they could finally stop hiding from the world. They'd lived and operated as an isolated team for so long, but he had never realised how significant and valuable their support network and resources really were to him.

* * *

45 hours later -

The men of Corwin's platoon lay about a bunkroom in a POW camp. They had no idea where they were, nor the location of the women, but Corwin had no fears for their health. He knew they were tough, and he trusted the Allies to look after them, no matter how crazy their story seemed. The group had barely spoken any words since arriving. They were waiting for something, they just didn't know what, but they knew they were unusual enough that eventually some questions would be asked. Finally, the call came.

"Sergeant Corwin!"

He stood up quickly to see two guards at the door waiting to escort him out.

"Don't fuck this up," said Porter.

Corwin nodded in appreciation of the helpful comment and carried on. He was led to the entrance of the camp and passed many German and Italian POWs, all still wearing their uniforms, only stripped of any Nazi related insignia. Not one of the enemy had spoken to them since they arrived. They looked intimidated by the physical size and strength of Corwin's squad.

He was show into a brick building at the entrance gates where he knew the commander of the camp resided, but instead he was led to another room in the same structure. It was a small interrogation room where a British officer sat waiting for him. As he stepped inside, a guard pulled shut a heavy barred security door and locked it. The officer was sitting casually and comfortably before him, and bore the rank of Captain. He looked inviting and friendly, gesturing for Corwin to step inside and take a seat at the table across from him. He was shocked by Corwin's muscular physique and kept looking back through a small paper file in front of him. He stuttered as he began to speak.

"I...I...I am Captain Hotwell."

"Sergeant Corwin," he replied politely.

"Yes...yes...I can see that in your file. What I am trying to understand, Sergeant, is not what your name is, but who you are. The story of your capture is most unconventional. I have a report here from a Captain Reeves to say that you and your comrades captured a German command post by yourselves and with no casualties. But then you could not identify yourselves and entered into combat with his men, but that you did so without the use of lethal force. You never fired your guns, why?"

Corwin raised his eyebrows, as that was an awful lot of information he had brought up, so he just focused on the last question.

"Because we are not the enemy."

"I really want to believe that, Sergeant. But you must understand, you were caught in enemy territory during a mission of vital importance. Yet the Americans have never heard of you, and they assure us they had nobody operating in the area."

Corwin took in a deep breath. He had been playing this situation out in his mind for days, but he still couldn't find the right way to do it.

"I can keep feeding you bullshit, or I can be straight with you, but you're not gonna like it."

"Let me be the judge of that please, Sergeant. Give me the facts. Who do you work for, what was your mission, and why have you not identified yourself if you are indeed an ally?"

"If you're willing to hear this, then I will tell it to you straight, but let me finish before you begin to doubt my story."

"Go on." He sat back to listen intently.

"The simple fact is this, we were there to hunt down the most dangerous man in the world; a man who should not be in this time and place, just as we should not be either. You cannot find record of us, and we cannot explain that because we were not born in this age, not in your lifetime, or anyone else alive here in this world. I never thought any of this possible until we arrived here."

Hotwell looked both completely confused and enthralled all at once as Corwin went on.

"A few days ago we were close to ending the world war we knew, until the leader of the enemy forces did the most unlikely of things. He travelled through time, and we went after him to try and stop him."

Hotwell was shaking his head and smiling now.

"Time travel? I didn't take you for much of a reader, Sergeant, but I think you might have been delving into fiction a little too much of late."

"I told you I would give you the truth, not that you would be ready to hear it."

That made Hotwell curious, and he leaned in across the table.

"Okay, I will play this game to its end, and then we will get the real truth. What year have you come from?"

"2074," Corwin replied quickly.

"And in this 2074, what are you?"

"Sergeant Corwin, Second Platoon, 1st Battalion, 12th Allied Infantry Division."

"From what nation do you hail?"

"As an Allied Division, we are drawn from many of the Allied powers. What you know today as America, Canada, United Kingdom, France, Germany, and many more."

Hotwell squinted as he racked his brain and thought about it.

"France and Germany, allies?"

"Is it so hard to believe that in over a hundred years, things might have changed a little?"

"No, what it is a little hard to understand, Sergeant, is

how you can feed me these outrageous and preposterous fantasies, and expect to be taken at all seriously. What else has changed in the hundred years since your time? Can men fly without engines, and do you live on the moon?"

Corwin shook his head. "Then what do you believe I am?"

"My best guess would be a spy. I believe you staged the deaths of the German officers you were found beside, and attempted to infiltrate our armies to some malicious end. And I believe you are now trying to feed me tall tales so that I will rightfully dismiss you as crazy and stop digging into the real story. Well, I am here to tell you, Sergeant, I will not stop digging, and I will not stop asking these questions until I get the answers that I am satisfied with."

"Then we will be here a long time."

"Okay, Sergeant, I will give you one opportunity to prove to me that you are indeed telling the truth and are not of this time. Prove it."

Corwin thought about it for a moment.

"Me and my people, we are not any ordinary soldiers."

"Go on?"

"We are what is known as Augmented and Psychologically Enhanced Servicemen."

"And what does that mean?"

Corwin looked around the room and to the heavy door barring the entrance.

"Could any human open that door without touching the lock?"

"Not with force, no," he replied confidently.

"May I?"

Hotwell nodded in agreement and sat back to watch out of curiosity. Corwin got up slowly and stepped up to the door. He placed a hand at either side of the door and gripped tightly before applying force. Brickwork splintered as the mountings were torn from the wall, and the door and frame from their position in one. He threw it down against the wall. The heavy iron made a crash as it landed and echoed down the corridor. A few seconds later a guard appeared before them with a submachine gun in hand.

"It's okay!" Hotwell shouted.

The guard looked at the damage in amazement and went to go onwards in Corwin's direction, but the Captain had his hand up to stop him and leapt across the room to stand between the two.

"We're fine here. Now leave us."

The guard looked highly uncomfortable as Hotwell ushered him out the doorway and sent him packing, and he turned to see Corwin had sat back down casually. Hotwell took up his seat again and stared at the Sergeant for a few moments, contemplating what he had just experienced.

"You've got me curious, Sergeant. Clearly, you are a lot more than you seem. But I still have no reason to believe the more than farfetched account of how you got here."

"And how could I convince you?"

"If you really are from the future, then you must be able to predict events before they happen, must you not?"

Corwin sighed and shook his head.

"Even if I knew that much about this time, and one of my team does, it has already been changed. The villain we followed to this time arrived sometime before us, and events are already unfolding differently than we know in our history."

"Well, isn't that convenient?" Hotwell asked sarcastically.

"No, it is a goddamn nightmare," replied Corwin sternly, "You have no idea what you are dealing with. In my history, you won this war. But the villain we tracked here, he can, and already is, turning the tide. If you do not set us free, and help us to complete our mission, this war could already be lost."

Hotwell took a deep breath and thought about it all.

"You know I thought I had heard it all? But time travelling super soldiers? No Sergeant, you are a spy, or some sort of clandestine agent or another. Maybe you are physically enhanced beyond the strength of any normal man, but by who and why, I wouldn't like to say. We aren't done here, but we are for now. I have better things to do with my time than discuss such nonsense. Real work and real intelligence gathering to do," he said, pointing to the door for Corwin to leave.

"You're making a huge mistake."

But Hotwell would not look at him. "Guard!"

Corwin got up to find the guard already at the entrance waiting for him, as he had clearly not gone far. The man led him out of the building and into the main yard.

"Time travel? What on earth have you been drinking?" joked the soldier, leading him on at gunpoint. Corwin looked around to see the smile on his face and then turned back to find a soldier standing right in his path. He was a tall and well-built German, the largest he had seen, matching Corwin in size. His head was shaven, and he wore a faded and scruffy field grey uniform. He had two scars on the left side of his face and was looking at Corwin with disgust.

"You are not one of us," he stated in a thick German accent.

"No shit," replied Corwin.

"Not one of us, what are you doing here?"

"That's a good fucking question."

He tried to step past the man, but he held out his hand and placed it against Corwin's chest to stop him, taking a pace in front of him once again.

"Then you are not welcome here," he stated grimly.

Corwin laughed.

"Not welcome? It's a fucking prison, why would anyone want to be welcome here?"

"He wants to fight you," said the British guard behind him, stepping further back and obviously waiting for the action to unfold.

"You don't want this," Corwin said to the German.

But without warning, the man swung a heavy and clumsy hook towards his head. Corwin took a step back with his right leg to plant himself, holding out his left to catch the fist mid air. The powerful strike was stopped dead with no effort at all, and the man looked terrified. Corwin replied with a straight punch from the right that hit the man in the face, launching him three metres back and off his feet. He tumbled to the ground as a lifeless mess. One of his comrades jumped to his side to feel for his pulse but shook his head in disbelief.

"Dead," he muttered.

Everyone looked at him in horror as some kind of freak, but the British guard was taking him seriously now.

"All right, move!" He pushed Corwin with the barrel of his gun to keep going. He was led back to his bunkroom. He stepped inside to see that his comrades had not moved an inch since he left. Though it didn't surprise him, as they had nothing to do with their time.

"Did you make any progress?"

Corwin shrugged.

"I made a few points that can't be refuted, Beyett, but how do you prove our story? I wouldn't have believed it, so why would anyone else?"

"Says the man who got us into this," said Porter, "We should never have given ourselves up."

"That the case or not, we are here now, and we must make every attempt to win the support of the Allied forces. We need their help as much as they need ours. They just don't know it yet," added Beyett.

"So what do we do?" asked Corwin.

"What we are already doing. We remain honest, make no attempt to escape, do not harm any Allied servicemen, and do not associate with the enemy."

"I don't think that'll be a problem." Corwin thought of the German he had just killed.

CHAPTER SEVEN

Two weeks later.

Corwin strolled through the camp. It was the most exercise they could hope for, and they were all anxious to get out and back on mission.

"Any news?"

"The operation in and around Dieppe that we got drawn into," said Beyett.

"What of it?"

"It's failed. I don't know exactly how badly, but the Allies failed to gain a beachhead and were forced to withdraw across the Channel."

"But it went a lot better than the Dieppe raid you remember?"

"Yes," replied Beyett begrudgingly.

"So what's the problem?"

"As I said, I think this version on the Dieppe raid was something of a cross between what happened, and the D-Day landings of next year. With the Soviet Union about to fall, the Allies must have pushed their plans ahead and tried to make some headway into France."

"And now?"

"Dieppe was a necessary tragedy that provided many lessons for the D-Day landings. I fear this is just a simple tragedy. With the Soviet Union gone, the Germans will have substantial resources to send this way."

"You're full of good news," Nylund said, walking behind them.

"Sorry, but I am only telling you the facts."

"And now, what do you think will happen from here?"

Beyett shrugged.

"Come on, you know better than any of us."

"One of the biggest disappointments of Hitler's time in power was that he could not carry out his treasured operation Sea Lion."

"Sea Lion?" asked Corwin.

"Some ridiculous attempt at a seaborne assault on England early in the war. But without air supremacy, it was doomed to failure. Again, with the Soviet Union defeated, and with whatever magic Villiers is working, I have no doubt we will see that operation come to fruition."

"Then this is a lot worse than we could have expected."

"Oh, yes, have no doubts, the safety of the free world never knew this danger. We may be all that can turn the tide now."

"No pressure," joked Corwin.

"Think about it. Nothing positive has changed for the Allies. But the Axis have gotten powerful enough to destroy one of the Allied nations this early in the war. Unless something changes drastically, I can see no hope of victory. We are all that can change the fate of this war now."

"The Allies did first time around, though, how are you so sure they can't this time?" asked Nylund.

"He's not. He's just taking a guess," Porter joined in the conversation.

"Yes, nonetheless an educated one," added Beyett.

"Still not getting anywhere with the Captain?" asked Harland, "I'm surprised they haven't resorted to torture yet."

"Be thankful these are better men than we ever were," replied Beyett.

"Every day he asks me the same questions, and every day I say the same thing in a different way. He thinks he is going to catch me out somehow, not understanding every word I speak is the truth."

"Then you need to find a new way to explain it."

"I don't think your methods on tact and diplomacy are anything I want to take from, Porter."

Another three weeks passed, and they heard and saw nothing new. The interned prisoners didn't dare utter another word to them after the death of one of their own at Corwin's hands, and the camp guards treated them with just as much suspicion. They were starting to lose hope, morale, and their minds. It was just after midnight one night like any other. All lights were out, but few were asleep; just Hunter who seemed to manage to sleep whenever he pleased, and as much as possible.

"We're never getting out of this hell are we?" Nylund asked, as they all lay in their beds dreaming of better days.

"At least nobody is shooting at you."

"Tano, I'd take that any day over this," said Nylund.

His voice was a little shaky, and Corwin understood how he thought. They all felt trapped and hopeless.

"We're the strongest resource these allied armies could ever have hoped for, and what do they do with us? Fuck all!"

"Our time will come, Porter," Beyett said.

"Hope so, because it doesn't sound like time is on our side," Nylund muttered, "Something has to change."

They all went quiet. But just ten seconds later they heard the crack of automatic gunfire, and a grenade explode not far from their position. They leapt from their beds and rushed for the windows.

"Careful what you wish for!" Corwin shouted.

They watched and waited. All hell seemed to be breaking loose as more guns joined in with the skirmish.

"Any thoughts, Beyett?"

"Why the enemy would be attacking a POW camp?"

Corwin nodded.

"Must be someone pretty important for such an operation on English soil."

"What are we going to do, stand by and let is happen?"

"Fuck no, Harland," replied Corwin, "This is our chance. Follow me."

He strode to the door of their block and kicked it full force. The hinges buckled, and the whole door flew off in one piece, striking the block opposite them. He stepped out to find a German soldier running towards him. He spun and grabbed the rifle, smashing his hand into the man's knees so that he flipped over and landed hard on his back. Corwin proceeded to stamp on his face and crush his skull. He then took the submachine gun from the corpse. He threw the weapon to Porter, who was next out of the door, and turned to carry on.

Porter ripped the webbing pouch belt from the man's

body and smiled. "This is more like it," he stated with glee.

Corwin reached the end of their building. Three camp guards were firing on the oncoming Germans, but were overcome by POWs that had escaped from one of the nearby buildings. Light machine guns were firing from two towers further into the camp, but the gate towers were smouldering and quiet.

The building where he had been interrogated in was about to be breached by several German soldiers. They'd blown the door off and threw in several grenades.

"Porter, Beyett, you're with me. Everyone else split up and get to work!"

He knew that was all the information they needed, as almost everyone in the camp was an enemy to them now. As they approached the front building, they heard the echo of automatic fire from inside. Corwin ran for the door at a full sprint and jumped inside without any care or caution. He had seen three enemy soldiers enter. The gunfire had stopped momentarily, until he heard three lower calibre pistol shots ring out.

"Lay down your weapon!" a German voice called out.

Corwin passed the camp commander's office to see he was slumped dead over his desk. He took a bend; the three soldiers were waiting to breach Captain Hotwell's office. Another shot rang out from a pistol inside the room, as one of the Germans pulled out a grenade. Corwin rushed at the man at full speed, hitting him so hard they barrelled through the single brick wall and thundered into the office, to the surprise of the Captain. Corwin grabbed the man by his helmet and smashed his neck down against the side of the desk to break his neck.

He then picked up one of the bricks that had landed

on the desk and threw it full force at one of the other Germans standing in the doorway. It hit him in the nose and broke it, blood spewing out over his face as he staggered back. The next raised his weapon to shoot, but two shots rang out from Hotwell's pistol, and the soldier was hit in his arm twice, forcing him to lose grip on his rifle and stumble back beside the other.

Corwin did not waste this opportunity. He jumped forward and grabbed the barrel of the gun of one and put it against the thigh of the other before squeezing the trigger. Three shots ripped through the man's leg as he collapsed to the floor. Corwin then smashed the stock of the rifle into the man still carrying it until he released his grip through the pain.

The Sergeant spun the rifle around and fired a burst into his chest, but the body armour took it all, so he raised the barrel and put one between the eyes. Finally, he turned back to the other. He was reaching for his weapon that had fallen out of reach but was unable to move as he was bleeding out. Corwin kicked the rifle out from his reach, placing his foot over the wounded leg and applying pressure. The soldier screamed in pain, but it was drowned out by the gunfire outside.

"Who are you here for?" Corwin shouted.

But the man only screamed in pain once again. He released pressure.

"Who are you here for?" he asked more calmly.

Corwin placed his foot above the wound and threatened to stamp on it once more.

"Okay, okay," the man pleaded, "Please."

"Start talking. What are you here for?"

"Corporal Winter."

"A Corporal? How can one Corporal be worth all this?" Hotwell asked, stepping up to Corwin's side.

He said nothing, and Corwin began to apply the lightest pressure on his leg.

"Okay, okay!"

He took his leg away and waited. The man took a deep breath and knew he had no choice but to let it out.

"He is Ubermensch."

"What the fuck is that?"

"Supermen…" replied Hotwell.

Corwin could already see where this was going. He was all too aware of the levels Villiers had gone to enhance his soldiers like the A.P.E.S.

"Why is he so fucking important?"

"He is one of the first in a new army that will be unstoppable."

"How was he captured?" Corwin asked Hotwell.

"In Dieppe like you, but I don't know how."

"Probably put into the fight to test his abilities. Losing a test subject like that must have been a kick in the teeth."

"Why?"

"Because of pride, you see what this man thinks of this Corporal Winter. I bet they have paraded him around as the next hero of the German people. How embarrassing do you think it must be that he is stuck in a POW camp?"

"They are doing this all for one man?"

"No, for one idea. If the Allies discovered who he was, it could be embarrassing."

They both looked to the wounded man on the floor, and he seemed to nod in approval. Corwin raised his rifle.

"No!' Hotwell yelled.

But it was too late. Corwin squeezed the trigger, and

a single shot went into the man's forehead just below the line of his helmet. He died instantly.

"Sergeant, you can't just kill unarmed men, whether they are the enemy or not."

"Yeah, well I just did."

Hotwell was too intimidated and thankful for his help to argue. He cracked open his revolver and loaded in six fresh bullets.

"You're gonna want something a little bigger than that." Corwin picked up the submachine gun from one of the other bodies and thrust it into his arms.

"What are you doing?"

"They want to get that superman out of here, you want to let them get away with it?"

Hotwell shook his head. "No, but, but…"

"But what?"

"I am not a field officer. I've never even had to discharge my weapon outside of training."

"Yeah, well time to break that cycle. Man the fuck up, and let's go."

He stripped all the magazines he could from the bodies and rushed on out of the building. There were four bodies at the door and Porter stood triumphantly over them.

"What's the plan?" Beyett asked.

"You familiar with the term Ubermensch?"

He nodded.

"Yeah, well there was one in this camp, and they're trying to bust him out."

"Villiers must be at his old tricks."

"No surprise there," replied Porter.

Gunfire rang out in the distance, and they could see two trucks tear off down the main road. Several camp guards fired on the vehicles as they fled.

"Fuck, they must already have him." Corwin turned to see the rest of his team had returned. There was still occasional gunfire in the camp as prisoners with liberated weapons tried to fight the camp guards, but that was of no concern to Corwin. He looked over to see two Willys jeeps parked at the entrance.

"Come on, I won't let them get that son of a bitch!"

The others had no idea what he was talking about but followed anyway. He leapt into the driver's seat of the nearest one, and Hotwell followed. He couldn't bear to be left alone with the enemy still roaming the site. He jumped in the back with Beyett and Hunter.

Corwin looked at the dash before him. It was simple, but alien to him. He could see an ignition switch and turned that on, but nothing fired.

"How the fuck do you start this thing?"

"Floor switch!" Hotwell shouted.

Porter looked around until he saw it and stamped on it until the engine fired to life. Corwin slammed it into reverse and put his foot down. They rocked back and stalled.

"Fuck sake!"

He reached over and hit the floor start again, put it into gear, and floored it. They rocked slightly with his poor clutch control, but finally the rear wheels spun in the dirt, and they launched forward.

"Never driven a classic?"

"Not in a while, Porter!"

He looked in the side mirror. Harland had got the other and was just a few vehicle lengths back. They were running without any lights at all, but could see the white convoy light on the diffs of the lorries in the distance. They bumped up and down over the rough ground and could barely see where they were crossing, but Corwin refused to slow down.

They were slowly closing the distance with the two trucks. Porter rested back and kicked the windscreen frame. The hinges locking it in place sheered off, and it smashed down onto the bonnet block; one of the panes shattered. He took aim with his rifle. All he could see was the silhouette of the canvas above the convoy light.

"You ready for this?" Corwin asked the three in the back. They nodded, but Hotwell was happy to sit back and watch as they went to work. He clenched the submachine gun tightly but couldn't bring himself to use it. Corwin put his foot down on the gas a touch further, and they soared forward a little more.

"Light 'em up!"

Porter, Beyett, and Hunter opened up on with bursts of full auto fire from their captured weapons. They noticed two of the enemy soldiers fall out the back as they were hit by the gunfire and tumbled out. One of them was clipped by the front wheel of their vehicle and caused them to slide slightly off to one side. Corwin reverse steered to get the power down, just about maintaining control as the gunfire sprayed all over the place.

Finally, they were back on track, and Porter was taking well-aimed shots at those ahead. A few shots came back their way, but the vehicle ahead suddenly slid sideways and overturned. It rolled several times as Corwin slammed on the brakes. Their jeep pulled to the right and went into a slight slide, as they ground to a halt in front of the wreckage. The moment they stopped, Corwin leapt out from behind the wheel and jumped forward. He cleared several metres and landed precisely on the side of the overturned truck. The canvas had been torn off, and the bed was filled with bodies. Only one seemed to be moving. He took aim and fired a few quick shots to finish him.

Gunfire rang out, and he turned to see Porter firing into the cab. The jeep engine revved up, and the vehicle pulled past the wreckage and stopped beside them.

"Come on, get in!" yelled Hotwell from the driver's seat.

They leapt in and the wheels spun as he raced onwards.

"How'd you know Winter wasn't in there?" asked Corwin from the front passenger seat.

"I don't, but they're all dead, and we'll have plenty of time to check afterwards. We let that other vehicle get away, and they could well succeed in their mission."

Corwin nodded in agreement as those behind them reloaded their weapons. The convoy light of the other truck was a faint dot in the distance now, but Hotwell was racing at the same breakneck speeds Corwin had been doing. He was hanging on for dear life and could feel the back wheels slide out every few seconds. It was like they were running on ice.

"They must be heading for the runway. It's not far from here," added Hotwell.

The concept of dedicated landing strips was alien to the others, but a novel reality that they were glad of on this occasion.

"A military airstrip?" Corwin asked.

"Barely. It was private, commandeered by the RAF, and protected by three guards at the most. I have seen what you are capable of, but do you think you can handle this superman?"

Porter laughed. "He's a school boy compared to us."

"For a man who never saw action, you sure are keeping calm, Captain."

"That is our way. It is the only way we know how."

They covered another few hundred metres and finally could see the silhouette of a large transport plane in the distance.

"C47, that must be their ride out of here."

"That's one of yours, isn't it?" asked Beyett.

"American. The Germans are getting pretty ambitious if they are encroaching on English soil like this."

"In a way that never should have happened."

They closed the distance quickly and could see the truck parked up beside the aircraft as the twin engines roared to life.

"Whatever happens, do not let that plane get off the ground," Corwin ordered.

They got to one hundred metres away, and the aircraft was in full view, though the truck blocked line of sight to the side door. Porter took aim at the cockpit and fired bursts from his assault rifle. He quickly emptied a full magazine and rushed to slam in a new one as the plane began to amble forward.

"This is gonna be close!" yelled Corwin, "Put your foot on it!"

The three in the back joined in the shooting, and they could hear more fire coming from the vehicle behind them as shots zipped overhead. The fuselage was riddled with bullets as they rushed onto the airstrip flat out. They were doing just sixty miles per hour, but it felt terrifying. They were closing the distance when all power was put down to the engines of the aircraft, and it began to open up.

"The engines!"

They took aim at the left wing side engine, firing with everything they had until at last it burst into flames. A large plate of metal flew off the top and rushed past Corwin's head as they began to close on the aircraft. They got within a vehicle's length when the British officer looked to Corwin for answers, as he was all out of ideas. Corwin looked back to the others and spotted two stick grenades stuffed in to Porter's waistband.

"Hand them over!" But he reached in and took them, anyway.

"Get me closer!" They raced up beside the tail, and Corwin stood up on the seat and leapt without any thought or consideration at all. He hit the rudder hard and slipped back about to fall, but he grabbed hold of one of the elevators with his free hand. He hauled himself up onto the tail wing and unscrewed the primers of both grenades.

To Hotwell's amazement, Corwin punched through the side of the aluminium frame and created a perfect oval hole in which he fed both grenades, and then leapt back towards the jeep. He landed on the hood, and Hotwell immediately hit the brakes. The gap widened quickly as the miserly drum brakes brought them to a gentle halt. Corwin looked back as the two explosions erupted in the rear of the craft. The rear wheel was blown off with part of the tail wing, and the fuselage smashed down onto the runway; sparks flew and it acted like an anchor, causing the aircraft to go into a spin.

It did a one eighty turn before one wing tipped and smashed into the ground and was torn off. One of the undercarriage wheels buckled under the strain, and the fuselage slid along the strip, finally catching fire on coming to a standstill. The moment it had stopped, Hotwell put his foot down and rushed on towards the wreckage with the other jeep beside them. The side door to the plane was ripped off as they approached, and a man stepped out, carrying it as if it were no burden at all and tossed it off to one side.

"Corporal Winter, I presume?" Corwin asked.

He was a tall and strongly built man. He stepped out into the open ground between them, stopping as four more survivors clambered out behind him. They held their weapons up in surrender, but Winter still looked defiant. He carried nothing but his clenched fists and looked ready to use them.

"Put your weapons down!" Hotwell ordered.

"Not this shit again," muttered Porter. His finger had already half squeezed the trigger and was ready to gun them down where they stood.

"Don't even think about it," Corwin said sternly.

"So you're some kind of special?" Corwin asked Winter.

The German smiled slightly in response, inviting him to put his skills to the test.

"Let's find out just how special you really are."

Corwin passed his rifle to Porter and stepped forward empty handed. Winter smiled, as did the other Germans. They all knew his strength.

"You arrogant American. You know nothing of strength."

Corwin only nodded in agreement.

"If you can beat me, you're free to go."

"Fool!"

Winter went forward in a powerful stride and no care

for his life at all. It was obvious he had never needed to worry about those he had fought. He swung a heavy hook towards Corwin, but the Sergeant made no attempt to move. He threw up his left arm and blocked the mighty strike in its tracks. Winter's eyes widened in shock when Corwin struck him with a straight punch to the centre of the chest; launching him back into the fuselage with such power his body bent the metal panels where he landed. The rivets sheered as it collapsed in on itself.

Winter winced in pain as he felt the heat of the flames on his skin, but quickly pushed himself off the wreck and back into a fighting stance. The other German soldiers looked both stunned and terrified. Their superman suddenly seemed awfully human. He went forward at Corwin once again but was a little dazed from the first strike. He tried to jab, but Corwin went under and struck a heavy blow into his ribs and heard them crack. Winter buckled slightly at the hips, and Corwin launched himself up with a flying knee, lifting the man up off his feet and smashing him back down onto the strip.

He was still conscious but defeated.

"What are you?" asked one of the enemy soldiers.

"The real Ubermensch," he replied.

"So there are more like you?" Hotwell asked.

Corwin nodded.

"Something like it, yes. Villiers, the man who we came to stop, he will be all too keen to attempt to re-create the programme that spawned us. He's tried many times before."

"Successfully?"

That depends on your definition of the word," added Beyett.

"What do you mean?"

"Most of his test subjects died early. Some went absolutely psychotic. One we know became a monster that I wouldn't want to face alone. This is the most successful subject I have seen yet."

"And yet he was not able to defeat you?"

"There is more to winning a fight than just strength," replied Corwin, "But the last thing you want is the enemy getting these new soldiers in any kind of quantity. We need to shut this shit down."

"Are all men as vulgar as you in the future, or is it just Americans?"

Corwin had to look at Hotwell for a moment to see that he was joking; for his humour was drier than anything he was accustomed to.

"So where do we go from here?"

"Where do you want to go with this, Captain?"

"I believe you, and I trust you, but it will be hard to convince others of the fact. Technically, you are still POWs interned at a camp. As of right now, escaped POWs."

"Only while you say we are. Your job was to investigate our story. You have done so and know we are not the enemy. You can vouch for us. You have to. You know you need us in this war, so fight in our corner."

They heard the sound of engines from several trucks heading their way. Corwin took up his rifle and rushed to the cover of their jeep. The others scattered and did the same. They watched three vehicles and two jeeps racing into view, and dozens of troops unloaded before them.

"It's okay. They're ours," said Hotwell.

An officer approached them with several soldiers by his side, their weapons held at the ready. They were cautious, except for the officer, who was confident and unflinching.

Corwin lowered his rifle and stepped out with Hotwell to address the officer, who looked down at Corwin's attire and captured rifle, but seemed to show no expression at all. Then he turned his attention to the burning wreck of the C47. The flames rose high into the sky now, and he turned his attention to the German prisoners.

"Captain Hotwell, did any of the enemy escape your grasp?"

"No, Sir. With the assistance of Sergeant Corwin and his squad, we were able recapture Corporal Winter, their target."

He looked back and forth at the two of them and then to the hulking Rane behind them. The officer had a well-kept moustache, carried a swagger stick under one arm and a pistol on his webbing belt, but nothing in hand. He had an air of confidence about him but also looked to be a fair and just man, or so Corwin hoped.

"You were a prisoner in that camp, were you not?"

"Yes, Sir."

He looked over at the prisoners again and then back to Corwin.

"It rather suggests you were in the wrong camp. I am Major Williams, and I thank you for your efforts here," he said, offering out his leather gloved hand in friendship, which Corwin glad accepted.

"Captain, I suggest you sort these men some appropriate accommodation, and be sure to get them back to fighting fit. We need every man we can get in this war."

"Major, there is more at work here than it might first seem. Corporal Winter is a high value target, and also highly dangerous."

"We'll deal with him," he said, pointing for his men to detain the captured Germans.

Corwin turned to his squad, noting they were relieved to finally not be treated like the enemy. They loaded up into the vehicles and rolled on back to the camp. Several more trucks and British soldiers had got everything under control, but Major Williams wanted to inspect the scene for himself. He got out of his vehicle and addressed Corwin and Hotwell as they pulled up in the jeep beside where all the fighting had begun.

"Tomorrow morning I'll need you both to come with me to HQ. We're still trying to piece together exactly what happened here, and there will naturally be plenty of questions. But for now, I suggest you get some rest. Hotwell will sort you out. Captain. 0700, I want a full report."

But Corwin didn't look easy, and that surprised the Major.

"Sergeant, I would have thought you'd be all to thankful to get out of this place and sleep on a real bed?"

"Only when all of my squad is free and with me. We came here together. We fight together, and there is plenty of work ahead of us yet."

"Captain, have the rest of the Sergeant's men released immediately," he ordered.

"Sir, they're...they're.."

"They are what? Bring them here forthwith!"

"They aren't men," he finally replied.

"What do you mean?"

"Major, if I may?" asked Corwin.

He nodded for him to go on.

"Sir, we are not a conventional outfit, as you may have

already noticed, and among our ranks were three females."

"Combatants?"

"Very much so."

The Major was shocked and lost for words for a moment, but then turned to Hotwell.

"Do you know the location of these three women?"

"Yes, Sir."

"Then take the Sergeant there, and you have them released immediately on my authority."

"Yes, Sir," he replied happily.

The Major carried on his tour as Hotwell turned to address Corwin.

"Well? Where are my girls?"

"We can't reach them by night. I will take you there tomorrow and ensure they are released, just as soon as we have briefed the Major."

Corwin said nothing. He only glared at the Captain until he gave in.

CHAPTER EIGHT

0600

The sun was in the sky, but they couldn't see it for the thick grey cloud cover. They rolled up to the entrance to an old country estate in three jeeps, with Hotwell at the driver's seat of the lead vehicle. It was still missing its windscreen; the latches that held it up smashed from the night before.

"There are so few females interned in this conflict that many of them are housed here. It used to be a private zoo owned by one of the richest men in the country."

Just two soldiers stood guard at the entrance, and there was little sign of any fences. Corwin knew the three women of his squad could have escaped it anytime they wanted to, just as he could have in their prison. He nodded in appreciation, knowing they had followed his orders.

The vehicles rolled to a halt, and he was quick to leap out and head for the entrance. He'd buttoned up his short and close fitting camouflage shirt that displayed his rank. It was looking more faded that ever now, as he had lived in it since arriving.

"Identification?" asked one of the guards.

He turned and looked to Hotwell. He simply waved them through, and the guards stepped aside. The Captain led them to the head office. It was quiet, and no one was waiting to see the Camp warden. Corwin pushed the door aside and strode in with the Captain by his side.

"Captain Hotwell, good morning!" the warden behind the desk said cheerfully.

But Corwin interrupted the welcome.

"You have three of my team here. Release them now," he stated firmly.

"I am sorry, Sergeant, but I am not sure quite who you mean, and neither do I have the power to release prisoners," he replied, smiling.

"Start getting helpful," spat Corwin.

"Excuse me…"

"These are the orders of Major Williams," interrupted Hotwell.

The name drop brought him to silence as he turned back to Corwin.

"I don't even know of the inmates you speak of," he pleaded.

Corwin shook his head.

"Look at me, and realise that you do know. Came in from Dieppe engagement, bit weird and off, won't take any crap. You know exactly whom I am talking about. Trust me, they'd stand out here. Get them out here now," he said calmly.

"Sergeant, I cannot help you."

Corwin's calm nerves were gone. He smashed his fist down on the desk. The thick hardwood top cracked and split down the centre. His hand went right through, and either end rose up, splitting it in half. The warden rose back out of his chair and crashed into the bookcase behind him. He was red in the face, and his heart was pounding in his chest.

"Please do as the Sergeant asks," said Hotwell.

"I won't ask again."

The man nodded shakily and led them out of the room.

"Major Williams has already given me permission in person to remove the three prisoners from your facility that are under Sergeant Corwin's command."

He led them to a room where they found Chas and Vi playing with a deck of cards. They were as calm as anything.

"Where's Lecia?" Corwin asked sternly.

"She is in isolation. She has not got on well here."

"No shit. You cage a girl like that, and she'll go crazy. You ever try that with me, and I'll rip your head off."

The man looked terrified. He could see it was the truth. He led them on down a corridor, and out through the back of the building into the rear gardens, to a concrete structure with five doors. They were small cells.

"Oh, she's gonna be pissed," said Corwin.

"How do you mean?"

"Captain, how'd you think you'd feel spending a day in one of those?"

"Rather unsatisfied, I'd say."

Corwin smiled.

"Yeah, you don't want to even imagine how she'll be thinking right now. It'll be a miracle if she doesn't kill someone before we get out of here."

The warden signalled for a guard to open the locks of one of the cell doors, and it creaked as it slid forward. It was totally dark inside, and they could only just make out the silhouette of a figure sitting in the corner.

"Esperon, that you?" Corwin asked.

"You know how long you have left us rotting here?" she replied in a sullen tone.

"Too long."

She suddenly leapt forward and stopped just a few centimetres in front of the warden. He froze in fear, but she only glared at him without a word. There was murderous intention in her eyes, and she looked ready to tear him apart.

"Lecia, stop fucking around. Let's get out of here."

Her gaze turned to him before finally leaving the warden and heading towards Corwin's side.

"Weeks! Really?"

"Did the best I could do."

"Not good enough."

He nodded and smiled. "Yeah, I know."

They got out quickly and were in the vehicles in no time.

"You know the Major will never believe your story? You may have won his favour and his support, but it will be quick to diminish if you share stories of time travel with him. He has no tolerance for lies, and that is exactly how it will seem," said Hotwell.

"You still don't believe it, either?"

"I believe you are here for the right reasons, and I cannot see why you would fabricate such a story, but neither can I find any reason to quite believe it yet. I am just satisfied to accept you as allies and leave it there, but that will not fly with the Major. He will want answers, or you may well find yourselves behind bars once more."

"Got any ideas?"

"We're going to have to pass you off as an American Special Forces detachment. It is a semi truth that we might just pull off. Are you familiar with the OSS?"

Corwin shook his head.

"Office of Strategic Services, an American outfit started just last year. Their job is mostly intelligence and espionage, but still little is known of what they actually get up to. It would explain the females in your team, and stop the Major pressing you too much on the facts."

Beyett piped up from the back seat.

"And us being in that camp was no accident at all. It was part of our ongoing investigation into genetic enhancement of German soldiers, and you were aware of our operations from day one."

Corwin approved. "Truth woven into a pile of bullshit, I love it."

"Yes, that's good. Be sure your people all know the score, and this might just work."

"We're going to need you, too," added Corwin.

Hotwell looked surprised.

"You're the only one who knows and trusts us. We will need you to open doors for us. I want you attached to my squad."

"If you think you can make that happen, then I will be more than happy to provide my services."

They arrived at Headquarters with just two minutes to spare, and Hotwell leapt out of the vehicle and rushed to the door. It was clear he feared the Major as much as the enemy.

"Beyett, with me. Rest of you stay put, and make sure everyone knows the back story."

Corwin followed Hotwell into the house. It was a vast English manor and lavishly decorated, filled with uniformed staff slaving away at administrative work. He shook his head, imagining the boredom of what that must be like, and couldn't help but feel it looked much like their time in prison.

They reached Williams' office, and Hotwell knocked before entering. Corwin had been expected some collective of officers, but it was just the Major awaiting them. He sat smoking a pipe with a newspaper in hand, and looked as calm and relaxed as any man could hope to be. He put the paper down and pointed for them to take seats before his desk.

They sat down, and he studied each of them for a few moments as he smoked his pipe, quizzing them with his eyes.

"Sergeant Corwin. I know every Allied serviceman that operates in this district of mine, every one of them, except for you and your team, which is rather unorthodox. Please, fill me in."

Hotwell started to sweat and looked terrified, but Corwin was calm and quick to respond in a polite and courteous fashion.

"My apologies that we were unable to announce our presence to you earlier, Major, but our mission was, and still is, of the utmost importance and secrecy. No one since we departed the United States has known of this mission, except for Captain Hotwell, who was instrumental in discovering the identify and capture of Corporal Winter."

"And now that your mission is successful, what are your intentions?"

"It is not complete. There is no going home for us. But

I cannot disclose any more of our intentions at this time."

"And who do you report to?"

"In England, nobody. We work alone, and report only to the OSS directly."

"And I suppose you want my help?"

Corwin nodded. "I cannot begin to explain how vital our work is."

"Weapons, uniforms, transport, this I can provide for you, but I think you need far more than I have to offer."

"We will take anything we can get, and we will need some staff, capable researchers and analysts. People you know you can trust one hundred percent. We have a lot of work ahead of us, and we need a team that can back our corner."

Williams thought on it for a while.

"Officially, this should be taken a long way up the chain of the command. I don't have the authority to back such an endeavour. Unofficially, we need all the help we can get in this damn war. Tell me, will your work help us win?"

"We may be more vital than you will ever know, yes."

"Then I will give you everything I can. I don't expect to know operational details, but I do expect to see results if I am to continue assisting you. I want Hotwell to act as liaison between us."

"Thank you, you won't regret this, Major."

He got up and led them out of his office and down a corridor to a large set of double doors. He pushed them open and stepped inside to reveal a spacious games room with a billiards table in the centre.

"From now on, this room is yours. I will have all those I select for you to report here, and I will ensure that all staff are made aware of your position here. You will only answer to me."

Corwin nodded in appreciation.

"Then, welcome to the 7th Parachute Battalion. Officially, you will be part of my command staff. That will keep you out of trouble, but we'll have to get you looking the part," he said, smiling as he turned and left.

Corwin couldn't believe his luck. They'd just bullshitted their way into the good graces of a competent and decent officer. Twenty minutes later the whole squad were sitting about the billiards room. They'd waited so long to get free that none had given any great thought as to where to go next, but Beyett broke the silence.

"Villiers...let's stay on target. We need to know where he is, what he has been up to, what he plans to do next, and how we can get to him."

They all looked to Hotwell for answers.

"You're the intelligence officer," Corwin said, "Time to earn your pay."

Hotwell took in a deep breath, feeling the extent of the pressure and responsibility being placed on his shoulders.

"Who exactly is this Villiers?"

"Maximilian Villiers," replied Beyett, "One of the most intelligent, brilliant, and dangerous men of our generation. Once a key weapons developer for our side, he defected after the wrongful killing of his family."

"That is all you need to know of his back story," added Corwin, and Beyett continued.

"Villiers went on to become the key leader of the enemy forces, an axis of evil, much like those who are now here. He almost turned the tide of the war, but on the eve of his defeat, travelled back here to this time."

"But why? Why now?"

Beyett smiled and pointed to Corwin.

"What is it?"

"Well...let's just say it wasn't intentional."

"So what, you took a gamble, and this is where you ended up?"

For a moment he let himself believe everything Corwin and Beyett was telling him, but then the absurdity of their story struck home, but he didn't say anything.

"It's true that we came here by chance, and it could not have been a worse time and place for Villiers to end up. With his mind, intentions, and abilities, he can change the world forever. He already has."

"But why would he side with Hitler? What possible reason would he have to do that?"

"Villiers wants nothing more than to destroy the United States and her allies, and he will do absolutely anything to achieve that goal."

"That's it? He doesn't want power or wealth or anything, just to destroy?"

Corwin shrugged.

"The made a monster of Villiers, a monster that we had more than a fair share in creating, and now we must kill it before it destroys humanity as we know it," replied Beyett.

Hotwell was going pale again as he felt the heavy burden being placed on him.

"Then give me a couple of days. It isn't as easy as pulling out a few files. I'll do all that I can to try and help, Sergeant."

"Don't try, do. We've wasted weeks rotting away in cells. Now we need to make up that time."

"We're soldiers, not clerks. We need to be out there

tracking Villiers down."

"And where would you start, Porter?" asked Corwin.

Porter shrugged.

"We need information more than anything right now. Let's get to work."

A few hours later there was a knock on the door, and Nylund opened it to find a military tailor with a wheeled cart full of uniforms. He rolled the cart inside, and Nylund ran his hand over the coarse wool fabrics.

"You have got to be kidding me?"

Corwin grinned. "Got to look the part."

Three days went by, and the billiards table became a pile of maps and notes. They each now wore the complete wool suit-like uniforms that itched all over. Photographs and maps were pinned to three large boards either side of the length of the table, and four staff allocated to them were constantly processing file after file of paper documents. Beyett sat at one end of the table, seemingly in charge of the chaos, and he was racking his brains as he stared at one map for thirty minutes.

Corwin was slumped in a chair across the room and knew they had ground to a halt. He looked down at an aerial photo he had in his hands. It had been there five minutes, and he didn't even remember what he was looking for anymore. He threw the photo down on the table and stepped up to stretch.

"Enough!"

Everyone stopped what they were doing and looked to him. They all hoped he had some answer, but he was so far from it.

"This isn't working. We keep hammering away at this, and all we're doing is fucking with our minds."

"So what's the plan, Boss?" Chas piped up.

The three women were dressed in skirts and tunics marked up as motor transport. Vi and Lecia looked appalled by it, but Chas sported the uniform as if she was modelling it and glowed with a sexy smile on her face.

"Come on, we're getting out of here. We need to clear our heads."

He picked up his red beret from the table and walked out of the room without another word. The rest followed out of curiosity and went outside to the jeeps supplied for them. The sun was going down as Corwin jumped into the driver's seat of the nearest one. Hotwell leapt in beside him.

"Where are we going?"

"The team needs to let off some steam, or they're going to tear each other apart. Where can we get a drink around here?"

"Now you're talking," said Porter.

"Head out the gates, and take a right. I'll guide you from there."

The engines fired up, and they turned on the tiny blackout lights on the wings of the vehicles. They gave little more than a light haze around the front of the jeeps. They got out onto the country roads, and Corwin was relieved to feel the fresh breeze on his skin. It didn't feel sharp anymore. They were already becoming acclimatised to the temperate zone that was now their home.

"You got a first name, Sergeant?"

Corwin saw he was genuinely curious. He was really warming to Hotwell. He'd proven a valuable ally in an alien world.

"Wyatt."

"Like Wyatt Earp?"

"Yeah, what of it?"

"Coming all the way from the future, I'd expect something weird and wonderful," he smiled, "It's not a bad man to be associated with. Earp was a great American. The name's John, by the way."

Corwin appreciated him sharing such personal information. He could already tell in his time there that few people were on first names terms, except for long-term friends and comrades.

"You any closer to believing our story yet, John?"

He shook his head. "You know how hard it is for me to wrap my head around it? And that I cannot share this with anyone around me? You ask me to support a story so insanely far fetched that I might enjoy it, were it a work of utter fiction, but terrifies me to consider it a reality?"

"No, I can't, because I've never had to hear such a story and be asked to believe it. A few weeks ago, I thought time travel was something for dreamers and storytellers. I wish it were not the case."

"Assuming I do believe it all, why did you take that leap?"

"Because Villiers has to be stopped, and we were all that could do it. We were there at the very end with one opportunity. But it wasn't a difficult decision to make. We could make that jump, or die there and then with nuclear weapon that was set to detonate after Villiers had left."

"Nuclear?"

"You don't want to know," added Beyett, "Pray you never know. Though that will be a problem we will likely have to deal with if we survive long enough."

"So you had no choice but to come through? This or

death?"

"Yep, that's about the sum of it."

"Do you regret it?"

Corwin laughed. "This or death? Only a fool would choose death."

"Do you think you will ever see home again?"

Corwin thought about it for a while.

"I'm don't even know where that is anymore. We've been fighting across the world for so long, home is us right here. I'm not sure it matters where we are."

"Then who are you fighting this war for?"

He hesitated for a moment and then answered, "I was never great with history, but I know who the good guys were in this."

"And you are yet to discover the true extent of the evil the Nazis really are," added Beyett.

They rolled into a pleasant village that appeared untouched by the war, and Hotwell was quick to point out the first drinking establishment. They pulled up outside along a line of other jeeps.

"I'm afraid the area has been rather taken over by the Americans of late, but I suppose you'll fit right in."

It was an old pub called The Boar, and looked as though it had remained unchanged for a couple of hundred years. The front door wasn't even tall enough to let Rane through without him ducking under. Hotwell led them inside with Corwin close behind. As they stepped in, they found a dozen US paratroopers staring at them. A couple nodded to welcome the Captain who they clearly recognised, but they looked at Corwin and his lot with suspicion. Rane's size caused a few gasps, but it was when the women entered that a few wolf whistled, and several clapped with glee.

"I'm sorry, but this lot aren't used to seeing women in such an establishment. They might be a little rowdy," said Hotwell.

They looked over and saw Chas shaking her ass at them, smiling as she played to the crowd, but the other two looked less than impressed.

"You might like to keep the women close," he added.

Corwin smiled. "They can take care of themselves. It's them you should be concerned for," he said, pointing to the paratroopers.

Hotwell and Corwin pushed their way through to the bar, and the Captain put in an order without a word to the others.

"Evening, fella," said one of the American airborne soldiers to Corwin.

"Hi," he replied suspiciously.

"Billy Adcock, 82nd," he replied with his hand stretched out to greet him.

He spoke in a thick Texan accent and seemed friendly. He had Sergeant's stripes on his sleeves, just as Corwin did.

"Wyatt Corwin."

The man looked taken aback. "You're no limey."

Corwin looked confused. He had no idea what the man meant.

"Not an Englishman," Hotwell clarified.

"How'd you end up with this lot?"

"Beats me."

"So you coming with us on this operation?"

"Which operation?"

"Well, no one rightly knows, but it's coming. We've

been training for something all week, something big. I just figured you lot would have been in on it."

Corwin looked to Hotwell for answers, but he had none.

"Seen any action yet?" Adcock asked.

Hotwell passed him his drink, and he took the first sip as he nodded in response. It was a frothy and still dark beer. Entirely alien to Corwin's taste buds, and yet remarkably soothing.

"North Africa?"

Corwin sighed. "Amongst others."

"Jeez, you sure have got around. We've been here four months just waiting to get in this fight."

"Your time will come, Sergeant. It will for all of us. Let's not wish it any sooner than it needs to," replied Hotwell, walking past with a large wooden tray with full glasses for the rest of the team. Adcock looked surprised to see the only officer amongst them, both buying and carrying the round.

"Sure wish we had officers like you, Sir," he said.

Corwin patted the man on the back before following the Captain over to a couple of tables where the rest of them were sitting.

"They're gearing up for another operation? Must be something substantial," Corwin whispered to Hotwell and slid the glasses out to each of them.

"I've not heard a thing."

"If the Major wants us to share details with him, we need a little back."

"Lieutenant Colonel now. Williams has been acting CO for a few weeks. He just received confirmation of the promotion."

"Good, we need someone like that in our corner, but we also need in on this operation."

"What?" They heard Vi yell.

The bar went quiet as everyone turned to look at her. Corwin could see three of the paratroopers eyeing her up and discussing her hair and tattoo with such curiosity. She rose out of her seat with Lecia in support as they strode across the room to confront the three men.

"This should be interesting," Porter said, putting his feet up on the table and sitting back to enjoy the show.

The two stopped before the men and eyed them up and down. The three laughed and clearly had little respect for either of them.

"You've got something to say, let's hear it," said Vi.

One of them pointed over at Chas sitting on the lap of one of the paratroopers on a barstool.

"That's a lady. We were just trying to work out what you were."

"Too much for you to handle is what I am."

They laughed, but out of the corner of her eye, Vi noticed something interesting. Two of the men sat opposite one another with hands locked in an arm wrestling competition. She'd never seen such a thing before, and it got her curious.

"You see that?" she asked them as she pointed to the challenge, "I bet there's not one among you who could take me down."

The tallest among them laughed so loud he almost fell over. But Vi took a step back and hauled a table over in between them, grabbed a chair, and sat down.

"Come on, I don't want to embarrass you in front of all your buddies," said the man.

"You got any balls or not?" she snapped back.

He took a seat, but couldn't help but look back at his friends and laugh.

"Well, okay," he finally said.

They locked hands. He was firm like an anchor, but she kept a soft touch.

"On three," she said, "Three, two, one."

Her arm suddenly went rigid as he applied pressure, but he could not move her even a millimetre. He pushed and started to put his shoulder into it, but was getting nowhere but frustrated.

"Come on!" the others yelled.

He looked into her eyes, and she was cool and calm now. She slowly applied pressure against him, and he could do nothing to fight her as his arm slowly went further and further down at a slow and steady pace. He was breathing heavily and fighting her with everything he had, but she simply pushed his hand into the table with no effort at all.

The room was silenced.

"What the hell are you? Some kind of freak?" asked the defeated man. He could not believe he would have lost in a fair fight.

"If she's anything like that in the bedroom, then jeez," added another.

She could only smile in response. "You'll never find out," she remarked and stood up and embraced Lecia in her arms, ramming her tongue down her throat. It was an impassioned kiss, and the paratroopers were utterly stunned.

"This won't end well," Hotwell said in amazement.

"Get out of here, you dyke bitches. You're not welcome," said the paratrooper; still aching as much from his sore arm as his damaged pride.

He pushed the two of them, trying to usher them out the door, but Vi only took one prompt to lash out. She punched the man in the face and dropped him in one.

"Oh, fuck," said Corwin.

Six of the other paratroopers leapt to their friend's aid and tried to take on Vi, but they had no idea what they were letting themselves in for. One swung for her, and she ducked aside, driving a punch into his groin and throwing him back over one of the tables. It buckled under his weight. Another rushed at her, but Lecia kicked him in the face, and he flew back against his comrades. One rushed at Vi, but she stepped aside and launched him towards a front window. He crashed through the glass and tumbled out into the road beside the parked vehicles.

Seconds later they heard a siren ringing from on the street, and two American Military Policemen rushed inside with truncheons in hand. They froze for a moment, seeing the two uniformed women at the centre of the fray, and a number of soldiers scattered about the floor around them.

"What the hell is going on here?" yelled one of the MPs.

Hotwell was quick to rush forward to address him.

"Our American friends here got a little frisky with our MT girls. I think they bit off a little more than they could chew," he joked, trying to cool the situation down.

"They're dykes looking to cause trouble, and they're not welcome here!" shouted one of the paratroopers.

"Shut the fuck up," replied Adcock, striding forward as the highest rank among them. He pointed to the three men who had first drawn issue with Vi.

"These boys started it, and this is on them alone."

The MP turned to Captain Hotwell for confirmation, as he was the only officer present. He nodded in agreement, and the MPs grabbed the three men and hauled them out.

"Whoever, or whatever you are, I sure wouldn't mind having you on my side when we go into action," said Adcock.

CHAPTER NINE

Corwin awoke on a bed he didn't recognise in a room with the same architecture as the pub they were drinking in the night before. He tried to get up but noticed his head was throbbing. A noise beside him caused him to look over. Lecia was pulling on her underwear just beside the bed. She looked at him and smiled as if to say good morning, but never actually said it.

"Where are we?" he asked, rubbing his head.

"Still at The Boar. We never left."

He slowly hauled himself out of bed and found he was naked, but he didn't care. He noticed a stinging pain running down his back and looked in a mirror on the table at the foot of the bed. Deep cuts from nails had been clawed into his back from his shoulder blades down to the small of his back.

"Really?" he asked.

She shrugged. "Got to have some fun in this life."

He found it hard to argue with that and reached for his uniform. He was soon out the door and heading downstairs and past the landlord. He felt as though he owed him money, but he had no currency of any kind.

"Thank you," is all he could give as payment.

"No, thank you," the man replied with a mock salute.

"And I am sorry for the window. I will have it sorted."

"Captain Hotwell has already arranged everything."

He nodded and carried on out to find a solitary jeep left for them.

"You've put a lot of trust in that officer, a man we really don't know at all," said Lecia as they climbed aboard.

"I know. But he even more so in us than we have in him."

He fired up the engine, and they raced off back to their new home. On arriving, they could already tell something was going on. There were lines of trucks and several platoons of troops outside the main building. Corwin rushed through and grabbed Beyett on the way to Williams' office. He burst in and found him discussing something over a map with five other officers. He opened his mouth to speak, only to hold his tongue, realising how much he was overstepping the mark in the eyes of everyone there, except for the Colonel.

"Ah, Sergeant Corwin, I take it you have news. Please excuse us, gentlemen," said Williams to the others to save the situation.

They stepped out of the room, and Corwin shut the door behind them.

"Sergeant, while I am happy to support you in your endeavours, I cannot rightly have an NCO barrel in on my affairs."

"I understand."

"And as a result, I am giving you a field commission."

Corwin was shocked.

"I cannot very well make you a Second Lieutenant. It would not befit your age or standing. From now on, you will be a Captain in this Battalion."

"You have the power to do that?"

"You leave that to me. I'll have our tailor sort you out with the appropriate attire. Now what is it I can do for you?"

"There is an operation being planned, isn't there? Something big. A joint airborne operation with the Americans?"

Williams frowned at the news. "How do you know this?"

"Soldiers talk. They always do. Pretty clear something is going down."

Williams thought about it for a while and then nodded in agreement that he would share.

"It is no secret that our attempt to establish a front in France failed. Its failure was mitigated to the public as much as is possible, but nobody is under any illusion that we failed, and the Nazis have seized on this to begin a new drive against England, the likes of which we have not seen since 1940. But with the Russians out of this fight, attention is once more being turned our way. The threat of invasion is a very real one, but that is not our concern at this moment," he said and pointed to a town north of Paris.

"Creil. We have reliable intelligence reports that this is the site of a new super weapon believed to be codenamed V4. Initial reports suggest this weapon has the potential to launch barrages of missiles that could destroy military or civilian targets in such abundance and brutality that we could never have envisaged."

"V4?" Beyett asked; he sounded surprised.

"Yes, what do you know of it?"

"Nothing, nothing at all," he said, looking horrified. He glanced at Corwin, knowing Villiers had to be involved in some way.

He was very interested in Beyett's reaction.

"You tried hitting it from the air yet?"

"I've been informed that bomber command has been trying to hit the facility every night for the last ten days. US Air Force has been taking turns as well, but they're meeting increasing levels of resistance, and the structure seems buried well below the surface, where conventional bombs just aren't able to get the job done. I am told new weapons are being developed, but they simply aren't ready. Therefore a ground mission is being organised. So what do you say?"

"You want us in on this?"

"I'm asking you to volunteer, yes. I will not order you into this mission for I know you have your own orders. But intelligence gathering, sabotage and espionage, those are your specialties, and you might well get an insight into your target's work. What was his name again?"

"Villiers."

"Yes, like the engines. I shall not forget a second time."

"Could you give me a few moments, Colonel?"

"Of course."

He led Beyett over to a corner of the room, leaning in closely to talk in private.

"This might be some work of Villiers, but is us getting involved a good thing?"

"I don't know if it will help us get any closer to Villiers, but I do know we need to do everything we can to help the Allies, and we need to build their trust so that we can rely on them when the time comes."

Corwin nodded. "Okay."

They went back to the table and studied the map before them.

"We're in."

"My preference would be for a large scale operation, but while we might be able to get the numbers in, we have little way of getting them back out again. This assault will have to use a bomber attack as a screen, and must involve as few aircraft as possible. I intend to land four C47s here," he said, pointing to a perfectly smooth and flat field just a few klicks from the facility.

"How many men is that?"

"One hundred and twelve."

"And what sort of resistance to you expect?"

"Modest. The Nazis have become arrogant of late. They think they can't be touched. I intend to show them otherwise."

"You will be taking part in this personally?"

"I would not ask any man to undergo a mission I would not do so myself."

"And the 82nd, how are they involved?"

"This is not the only facility of its kind. We are part of a far larger operation, the scale of which is being kept even from myself. Allied commanders are afraid of leaks, and rightly so. The Dieppe landings were compromised in so many ways from the very beginning."

"So when do we go?"

"If the weather allows for it, in three days. Just know this. Once we get over France, we are what Hitler has called Clandestine forces, and there is a shoot to kill order on us all."

"It's nothing new to us," replied Corwin confidently, "I'll need some time to get my team together, and I'll need access to weapons and equipment. We can help you more than you realise, but we need to assemble our gear and do things our way."

"I'll make sure you have all that you require, providing I have your word that this operation stays strictly between us and your team."

"Of course, Sir."

"I will have someone along soon to help arrange your gear. Anything else you need, you let me know. It'll be an honour to have you with us on this one...Captain."

Corwin smiled. It had a nice ring to it. He'd never considered the possibility of being an officer, and yet it came at the most unlikely of time and place. They stepped out of the office and headed for their operations room.

"You, a Captain in the British Army?"

"Just when you thought things couldn't get any stranger, right, Beyett?"

He stepped into the former billiards room to find only Hotwell and his team of analysts were doing any work. The rest lounged about uneasily awaiting some action. Porter had his feet up on the table and was puffing away on a pipe he had liberated from god knows where. As he stepped into the room, they could all see the hope in his face and knew there was some news.

"We finally got a job to do?" Porter asked; the pipe still clenched in his teeth.

"Yeah, it's dangerous, with little support, and no backup plan."

"What's the bad news?"

"That we have to wait three days."

Several sighed in despair; they were anxious to do something and make some progress. He began outlining the operational details, but a few minutes later there was a knock at the door, and he moved to open it himself. He pulled it ajar to find a slightly portly and older Sergeant Major. He had a rigid and proud posture and held his chin high as to show off his grey moustache.

"Sergeant Major Wadd reporting for duty, Sir."

"What can I do for you, Sergeant?"

"It is what I can do for you, Sir. The Colonel has asked me to ensure you get everything you need."

Corwin smiled and turned around to his squad. They were more than a little curious.

"Time to up gun."

"Now you're talking," said Porter, finally putting his feet down and getting up with some enthusiasm.

Twenty minutes later they found themselves in an ordnance hangar with rack after rack of rifles, machine guns, and other assorted weapons. Vi stood in the open shaking her head at how antiquated it all was compared to what she was used to.

"This stuff is crap."

"For once you'll have to rely on something other than gadgets," said Harland.

"Hey, whatever does the job best," she snapped back.

"We'll just have to manage with what we can get," added Corwin turned to Hotwell.

"All our gear that was taken off us in France and beyond, can you get it?"

"It's already on its way."

They stepped forward to a table with a selection of equipment. The Sergeant Major first picked up a rifle with all wooden furniture.

"The staple of the British Army," he stated with pride as he racked he bolt action mechanism.

"Single shot?" Vi asked in amazement.

"Powerful, reliable, dependable. The well trained soldier can kill a man at five hundred yards with this fine weapon."

Corwin was shaking his head. "Need more firepower."

"I'll take a look," said Lecia.

She reached out for the weapon, but the Sergeant Major looked uneasy handing it over to a woman.

"Have you handled a rifle before, Miss?"

"One or two," she replied sarcastically, snatching it from his grasp.

"Sten gun," said Wadd, "Lightweight, easy to carry and use. It has a high rate of fire and is simple to maintain and operate; excellent in close quarters combat. Also available with integrated suppressor, which greatly reduces noise."

Corwin still looked unimpressed, though Frasi stepped up and took the silenced variant as the others went on. Corwin couldn't take his eye off a magazine fed light machine gun. The banana shaped magazine arose out of the top of the receiver to make a rather strange but oddly appealing design. He reached forward and picked it up off the table as if it weighed nothing more than a carbine. Wadd looked a little surprised but went along with it.

"The Bren light machine gun. Utilising the same potent .303 round of the Enfield rifle, the Bren is highly accurate and reliable, with sustained fire capability."

Wadd pointed over to a large open door to the side of

the building that gave access to an open range. Corwin pulled out the magazine, reached for a fully loaded one on the table, and then walked over to the range.

"The Bren can be fired from the hip position to provide suppressing fire on the move, but is best suited to use in a prone position, where its bipod can provide a stable shooting platform," said Wadd.

But Corwin slammed the magazine in and cocked the weapon, lifting it to the shoulder like he would a rifle. He held it in place with a perfectly calm grip, where any normal shoulder would be shaking in seconds. He squeezed the trigger and fired a three-shot burst at the twenty-five yard range target, then another, and another. Wadd looked in amazement to see a two-inch grouping sustained throughout.

"I must say, Captain, I have not seen that before."

"This will do as our standard rifle."

"Rifle? That is no rifle."

"Far as I'm concerned, this is an assault rifle. Have you not seen what many of the German troops are now carrying? They're ahead of the game."

"But the Bren is more for any one man to manage in that way."

"You let us worry about that."

He looked past the Sergeant Major to see Rane lifting a huge water-jacketed machine gun off the table. He couldn't help but think it looked like something from the nineteenth century, not the twentieth. The size and heft brought a smile to his face.

"I like this already," he said and hauled it over to the range, placing it down on the table.

"The Vickers gun, I must insist that you mount this on

a fixed platform."

Rane shook his head, and Wadd sighed in acceptance.

"May I?" Wadd asked.

Rane took a pace back as Wadd pulled out a metal ammunition tin and placed it beside the weapon. He opened the receiver and pulled an ammo belt from the box, placing it onto the breech before shutting the receiver and cocking the charging handle back. Wadd looked astonished when Rane picked up the weapon with as little effort as Corwin had handled the Bren. He held it at hip level and pushed the trigger. Light flashed from the muzzle as the gun fired into life. Its slow pulsing rate of fire kept going and going as Rane ripped several targets apart, finally stopping after fifty continuous shots.

Wadd couldn't help but look at the accuracy they had been fired at and marvel.

"That'll work, but it'll need a mount for the ammunition boxes, and a front grip. Something like that," he said, pointing to the wooden carry handle on top of the Bren.

Wadd looked at Hotwell for confirmation, but the Captain only nodded in approval.

"I will have it ready by the end of the day, Sir."

Vi picked up the Bren that Corwin had been using. She could handle the weight just fine, but she looked unimpressed by how unwieldy it was.

"Got something in between?" she asked.

"You ladies will not surely ever go into a combat zone?"

"We cannot give you operational details. Please just provide us with what we require," Hotwell intervened.

Wadd nodded, went over to a racking unit, and came back with a Thompson submachine gun. Most of them recognised it immediately. It was hard not to recognise the gun of all the gangster movies.

"Oh, hell, yes."

Vi almost swooned when she saw it.

"Firing the .45 calibre bullet, it packs a rather larger punch than our Stens," said Wadd.

In his other hand he carried three magazines.

"Twenty, thirty, and a fifty round drum magazine."

"Side arms?" Nylund asked.

"You sure are taking an awful lot of firepower for a twelve-man section."

"Yeah, well we punch above our weight," replied Corwin.

Wadd led them to a table of handguns. There were a few revolvers of varying size. Porter picked one up and looked at it and laughed out loud. He snapped open the barrel to reveal the cylinder for loading it and spun it with his fingers. He smiled like he was playing with a child's toy. Then he picked up the .38 rounds that it used.

"What are these gonna do, piss the enemy off?"

Corwin reached immediately for the Colt automatic, an icon he was at least familiar with.

"We'll take one of these each."

"Two for me," added Chas, picking up one in each hand and twirling them for fun.

"We're gonna need plenty of ammo. I'd say about three thousand rounds of the .303, two thousand of the .45, and two hundred 9mm."

"Are you intending on fighting this war singlehandedly?"

"You can never have too much ammunition," he replied.

"Americans," Wadd muttered. He shook his head and wrote down the figures on a notebook.

"Grenades?" Harland joined in the conversation.

"The venerable Mills bomb, how many do you require?"

"Four per man," Corwin answered.

"And the women?"

"Them, too. This supply will keep us in action for a day. Hopefully, that's all we'll need for now. If we're out there any longer, you know it all went tits up."

"Tits up?" Hotwell asked.

"It's what we'll be if this operation falls apart."

"Anything else I can do for you, gentlemen?"

"That'll be all, Sergeant," replied Corwin.

They stepped out of the building and headed on their way.

"What would you have me do in this operation?"

"You aren't coming with us, Captain."

"I won't? That's a relief."

"You're more valuable to us here. Keep working to find out when Villiers started showing up, and where he could be now."

"You think finishing him will make enough of a difference?"

"Yes, every day he helps the Nazis is another step closer to their victory. He must be stopped."

* * *

The day of the operation had finally come, and it was late afternoon when they stepped out into the courtyard of the building. Williams and his people were loading their gear onto a line of trucks. Many of the paratroopers stopped and stared at them. For all the uniform and discipline in how they wore it, Corwin's Luckers looked like a rag tag bunch of hooligans. Gone was the need to blend in; now they were ready for just one thing, a fight.

They each wore a mix of the wool clothing they had been supplied with, and elements of the equipment they'd brought back with them. Corwin had no jacket at all and had his wool shirt rolled up above the elbow, with his body armour over the top. On his hip he wore a Colt in a low-slung tankers holster, like a cowboy would carry a gun. In one arm he carried his new Bren gun, and in the other a Bergen chocked full of magazines for it.

Rane looked even more ridiculous. He had cut the sleeves of his tunic off at the shoulders and wore his armour over the top like the rest. He had ammo belts slung over his body, and a Bergen on with boxes of ammunition stuffed so high that they were almost sprawling out the sides of the lid.

Lecia's long form-fitting coat fluttered in the wind and had been re-sprayed a camouflage mix, not unlike the Denison smocks worn by the paratroopers. Yet she wore the British battledress beneath and carried her scoped Enfield rifle with two cotton bandoliers across her body. Her hair had been dyed a mix of brunette and green so that it blended into her jacket, as it had done before in the desert.

The British soldiers could not work out what they were looking at, or what the team had to do with them.

"Everyone listen up!" Williams ordered.

The Colonel leapt onto the bonnet of a nearby jeep so he could be seen and heard by all. He was in full combat attire with a jump helmet on and pistol on his webbing, along with pouches filled with Sten magazines.

"I want to introduce you all to Captain Corwin and his squad. They'll be coming along with us. They volunteered for this mission. They're somewhat unconventional, but my understanding is they can be more than a little help when you find yourselves in a tight spot. I am well aware that their inclusion in this mission, and in this Battalion, is a long way from protocol or tradition. But, gentlemen, we live in strange and dark days, and we must look for hope in all corners of life. I ask you extend them the same respect you would your fellow soldier. They are, after all, part of the Battalion now. Load up, and move out!"

He jumped off the hood of the jeep and rushed over to Corwin's side.

"Really think you can handle that gear? This is going to be a rapid deployment with vastly developing lines. We aren't in this for the long haul."

"Don't worry about it, Colonel. We are no rookies in this."

He led Corwin to the back of one of the trucks where he pointed to crate loads of explosives.

"Each platoon will carry enough charges to bring this structure down, providing we can reach structural supports. Trouble is we still don't know exactly what we'll find inside. Rule of thumb here, we take far more than we need, and blow the whole facility to kingdom come."

"My kind of plan."

I want your squad to work with two sections of my own boys, forming Seventh Platoon, A Company. They're good lads, and they'll appreciate your presence. As your commission is rather more symbolic than anything else, you will be under A Company's platoon leader. Lieutenant Burr. I presume that will not be a problem?"

Corwin shook his head.

"This is your operation, Colonel. We are just along to

help."

"Corwin, I know you have your mission to think about, but please, don't hold anything back. Your people know a lot more about the inner workings of what's going on over there than you let on. If you see or find anything that could assist us in this war, please share them with us."

"Of course. Ultimately we're only here for one thing, and that is to make sure the Allies with this war."

Williams smiled as he walked back around to the troops. "Load up!"

Just a few minutes later they were loaded into a convoy of eight trucks and four jeeps and hitting the road. Corwin's squad had a whole vehicle to themselves. It was a clattery and rickety truck that groaned as it hit any minor trough in the road. A few minutes into the drive they could hear the smattering of rain on the canvas overhead, and it wasn't long before water began seeping through a hole in the skin and drop in between them.

"This sucks, Boss," said Vi, "This ain't even our war. I don't know why we bother."

"Why did you ever sign up in the first place?"

She shrugged as she couldn't fully remember or understand why, but Beyett stepped in to reassure her with some hard facts.

"Do you know what the Nazis thought of homosexuals?"

She shook her head. "If it's anything like the fuckers we've met so far, I doubt it was too great."

"It's true that the Allies were often not kind, but the Nazis believed homosexuals were the lowest form of scum. I remember some quote from one of their key leaders as describing your kind as mentally diseased, cowardly, liars, traitors, irresponsible, and disloyal. They believed men and women existed to breed, and therefore homosexuals were a threat to society."

She spat on the floor between them, but Corwin could only smile, understanding what Beyett had done.

"They really are the bad guys, Vi," added Nylund.

"What the fuck would you know?"

She turned to Corwin to look for some confirmation.

"If Beyett says it is so, you better believe him. Everything I ever learnt about the Nazis tells me they are the real deal. Just the sort of scum we fought against, and if good men, and women, hadn't fought this war, we'd not have been able to ever fight our own. These are good people, and they need our help."

"They surely do, now more than ever," Beyett agreed.

They all thought on it for the rest of the journey, eventually arriving at the airfield. It was hammering with rain as they leapt out from the back of the truck and slashed into the surface water at their feet. Corwin looked up at the sky to feel the rain beating down on his face. It felt fantastically refreshing, and he could not look away. Not until he heard Williams' voice.

"This isn't going to work!"

Corwin looked over to the Colonel.

"We can't fly in this weather!" he shouted.

Corwin shook his head. It wasn't extreme enough to ever have affected an operation in his life.

"How long?"

But the Colonel only shook his head. He clearly had no idea and beckoned them to follow him to a nearby canvas shelter, and they rushed inside. It was a vast structure and filled with all those taking part, over a hundred soldiers. Corwin found a free space, threw down his pack, and lay down beside it. It was already dark, and they wanted to sleep, but were too high on the adrenaline that came with the opening of an operation to ever sleep.

"Little water and they shy away, pussies," said Porter.

Corwin looked over to see the most despicable of his squad was sitting opposite him, and then noticed Lecia beside him. He looked back to Porter and sighed as he thought of his negativity and nihilism.

"Why did you ever sign up to this, Porter?"

He laughed before responding. "Most fun you can have and get paid for."

"You don't believe in our cause, though? Don't believe in right or wrong?"

He laughed once again. "I know more than you will probably realise. I just see a bigger picture than most of you."

It was a disturbing thought, but Corwin was willing to give it a chance.

"You're beyond fucked, you know that?"

Porter only grinned at Lecia and gave her a mock salute.

"Come on, he's talking some sense. Let's hear what words of wisdom he has for us."

Porter drew out the pipe he had been smoking of late and continued to pack and light it while the two of them waited with some anticipation to hear what he had to say.

"Okay, so you keep fighting for some sense of what, honour? Duty? Humanity?"

"Something like that," Corwin replied.

"It's all shit. Society is fucked, and you have to accept it. We keep fighting for different ideals and realities, why?"

"Because one is better than another?"

"And you think I am fucked up?" he asked, laughing

again.

Corwin managed to smile at least, but Lecia looked less than impressed.

Time passed slowly, but they knew there was going to be no news as the weather progressed in the same fashion they had experienced. They awoke the next day and found nothing had changed. Corwin found himself standing at the edge of the canvas just centimetres from the rainwater still pouring down. Williams appeared at his side.

"I suppose you are used to waiting for these opportunities?"

Corwin shook his head.

"Seen plenty of combat, but never had to wait for it."

They waited out the rest of the day under canvas. It was the most boring experience the Luckers had ever had, unable to go anywhere or do anything. All they could do was wait where they were. The day passed slower than any week. They all knew the operation had to take place during nightfall. The sun was going down on the second day, and they were all awaiting news, when finally the rain came to a stop and they hoped for something.

Finally, at 7.30pm the Colonel rushed into the tent and yelled, "Fall in!"

Shouts of excitement from those inside echoed around the tent, but not the Luckers. They were keen to move on and do something, but were not excited at the prospect. None except for Porter, whose sick sense of humour warranted a regular portion of violence.

They grabbed their gear and rushed out of the tents to see the silhouettes of the C47s awaiting them on the airstrip.

"A chance to stick it to the Nazis? Never thought I'd

have the chance," said Nylund.

Nobody was sure whether he was putting on a show or not, or even if he really understood the conflict, but they were all starting to feel it.

CHAPTER TEN

They were fifty minutes into a forty-five minute journey. No one had said a word for the last thirty minutes. Corwin watched the British soldiers out of curiosity. He'd not had chance to say more than a fleeting hello to the young Lieutenant Burr. He looked little more than twenty-one years old. Despite his youthful looks, he had an air of confidence about him that Corwin admired, and that showed in how his men acted towards him. They were every bit as calm that he and his squad were, and yet he knew they could have seen little action. Many of them still looked at Corwin's group with suspicion, and particularly with doubt and amazement at the women in the group.

Porter had his usual wicked grin on his face.

"What are you so happy about?" Nylund asked.

"You lot seem to think it's some fucking tragedy that we're stuck here. All I see is a more interesting war, and more people to kill. This is what we were born for."

"You think fate got us here?" Tano asked.

"Why not?"

"Because if you believe in fate, you accept that we cannot have any effect on our deeds and actions, or any others. That we are merely playing out a script," added Beyett.

"Would that be so bad?"

"To know you are merely a puppet with someone else pulling the strings?"

Porter shook his head at Tano.

"Forever worrying what could be, why not just roll with it and enjoy the ride?"

Tano shook his head and didn't respond because he knew he wasn't getting anywhere. Beyett opened his mouth to speak but was drowned out by a hail of bullets hitting the fuselage of their aircraft. Machine gun fire strafed the length of the craft. One shot was stopped dead on Corwin's body armour, and another clipped Porter's left arm, causing a shallow cut to open. But it was the British sticks who took it the worst. They were riddled with bullets. Seven were killed outright, and another three wounded. A moment later they heard the sound of an aircraft buzz overhead.

Corwin leapt out of his seat and to the far side window to see for himself. A German fighter soared past and was banking hard to come around for a second run. One of the other C47s had been struck in its left side engine and cockpit. It was plummeting towards the ground. In that moment he realised just how mortal they were; they were not even carrying parachutes. Beyett was quick to rush to the aid of the wounded soldiers.

"What do we do?" Lieutenant Burr shouted to Corwin.

He could see the terror in the man's eyes, for they were indeed in a death trap.

"He's mine," stated Lecia.

She jumped over several bodies as she rushed to the back of the plane and pulled open the side door. Corwin and Burr ran to her side with weapons in hand.

"What are you doing?" Burr asked in amazement.

Corwin placed a hand on his shoulder.

"Let her work!"

They looked out; the fighter was still banking hard to come up on their tail where their unarmed transport would be a sitting duck. It came up on their rear left hand side, allowing all three of them to see it from the doorway.

"No way you can make that shot!" Burr yelled.

She clung to the side of the fuselage, locking her rifle against it for stability, and began to take aim.

"We can't take another pass!"

The fighter's guns opened fire, but only got off two shots as Lecia squeezed the trigger on her Enfield rifle. The shot penetrated the fighter's cockpit and struck its pilot in the forehead, killing him instantly. The gunfire stopped, and the aircraft began to bank and finally dip into a spin.

Burr was wide eyed in shock.

"How?"

But she said nothing in response. Corwin hauled the door shut, and they looked back to the stunned soldiers staring at them. Finally, one began to clap, and within a few seconds even the wounded had joined in. But she did not blush or look at all fazed by it. She stepped back to her seat as she passed the applauding solders.

"That's just showing off," said Vi.

The wounded were patched up as best they could. One looked close to the end, while the others seemed like they'd make it and were eager to go on, if not capable. Burr knelt down beside the two with lesser wounds.

"When we get to the ground, you two stay here, and look after him," he said as he pointed to the dying man.

It was an act of kindness towards all three of them, and Corwin was impressed. Nevertheless, they were rapidly losing combat strength. The pilot looked back at him with a look of dread.

"Undercarriage is damaged!" he shouted.

"Just do whatever you have to do to get us on the ground!" Burr ordered before Corwin could say much the same thing.

Everyone knew the plane was their ticket out of there, but they were too focused on the mission to let that get in the way. They were making their descent quickly now. In the distance they saw flashes of light from bombs lighting up the sky, and they could hear the continual thunderous eruptions as the RAF smashed the target they were heading for. Corwin looked out of the window. They were coming in fast, so he took a seat and braced himself ready for the impact. He reached across and took hold of one of the wounded men and held him firmly in place.

"Hold on!" yelled the pilot.

Part of the undercarriage that was down touched the surface of the field with an almost perfect landing. The pilot held it there and slowly brought the other side of the plane down until the wing clipped the edge of the field. It turned and slid in the mud. Half of the wing was torn off, and the undercarriage collapsed. The belly of the fuselage smashed into the dirt and brought them to a quick stop.

The pilot shouted, "Everyone okay?"

Corwin looked around and amazingly they were okay,

if a little stunned. He got up and rushed to the door.

"Get the wounded to one of the other birds."

"Stay alert, and stay safe," Burr said to the crew of the craft. He rushed to the side door and tried to force it open, but the fuselage had buckled and it was jammed.

"May I?" Rane asked.

Burr turned in surprise on finding the towering soldier standing right next to him. He stepped aside, and Rane kicked the door with seemingly little effort. The door buckled and folded at the centre, and then burst off its hinges. He flew five metres across the field and left Burr in utter shock. He thought to ask more, but stopped; he was just glad to have Rane on his side.

They leapt out of the aircraft and found themselves just thirty metres from the nearest friendly aircraft that had touched down safely. There was so much moonlight they could see clearly across the open field. That was both some relief and terrifying, for their approach to any enemy target could therefore be seen from a great distance.

Corwin noticed Williams approaching at the head of his platoon. They seemed to have made it to the ground unscathed. The CO looked at their wrecked aircraft and dwindling numbers for just a moment before realising the mission must go on. He looked around to get his bearings for just a moment before pointing and leading the way.

"Come on," he said and went enthusiastically forward.

Corwin wasn't sure whether he was a man with combat experience or just had an inbuilt and inbred confidence that made him endearing, but he'd gladly follow the Colonel. They continued on through the night with seemingly no resistance at all. It seemed to them all that they had made it there safely; they hoped at least.

After covering a few klicks through the countryside, they reached a main road leading to the target, and sharply deviated to the north to track through foliage and around a perimeter fence. Williams brought them to a standstill, and Corwin was close by his side. He was pointing to a guard tower with a sentry just the other side of the fence. A large spot lamp was mounted on the near side.

"Let us handle this," said Corwin.

Williams nodded in agreement, and Corwin pointed for Frasi to go forward. He slung his suppressed Sten over his body and covered the distance with such agility and finesse that he was barely visible as he hugged the ground. He reached the fence and scaled it more nimbly than a cat and was over it before anyone had time to notice.

Frasi seemed to vanish into the short foliage the other side of the fence, and everyone waited with anticipation. Then they saw him leap onto one of the support beams without even using the ladder. He stormed up the side and leapt through one of the narrow openings of the tower. He launched himself onto the guard like a bird of prey, and both collapsed out of sight. Just a few seconds later, Frasi appeared and beckoned them to join him.

Williams signalled them forward, and three of his platoon went straight for the fences with wire cutters in hand. They went at the steel piece by piece, but it was taking an age. Rane was getting tired of it and ran forward at one of the support beams. It was thick as a telegraph pole. Seeing his previous display of strength, Burr didn't question it and only watched in awe.

"What's your man doing?" Williams asked.

But Corwin only pointed towards the fence for them both to watch. Rane hit the post with immense speed and power, and it sheered at the base. Fifteen metres of the fence around him flattened as he smashed it down into the complex. He looked back at Corwin and wanted to speak, but knew they had no time, so merely signalled for them to go forward and advance through the opening that had been created for them.

Some distance away, fire crews were battling flames that the bombing had caused. There were large craters across the open ground, and several concrete domed structures appeared to be the roofs of the underground structure. Williams signalled for one of the platoons to circle off to the left hand side, and for Burr to go right. He took the centre.

The bombing had ripped a number of holes in the structure, with several car size pieces now scattered across the site. But most of the damage was merely to the ground around them, and repair crews were already at work fixing the damage. Frasi was still far ahead of them and approached the nearest crew with his suppressed submachine gun in hand. He opened fire on single shot without stopping and killed four of the Germans with eight perfectly aimed shots. They could barely hear the noise of the heavily dampened weapon. He stopped soon after, and as the rest of them caught up with him, they came across a ramp leading down into the facility. It had a two metre thick steel roof at the opening. There was a huge tear where a shell had clearly struck it and prised the metal apart, and yet not been able to damage the structure.

Corwin was first down the ramp, but Burr was close behind. The ramp zigzagged several times until they arrived twenty metres below the surface, where to their amazement they found an open doorway. As they approached, two soldiers appeared and stepped out before them. Both carried weapons on their shoulders and had no warning of their presence. They stopped and quickly pulled the weapons from their shoulders, but Burr opened fired with his Sten as Corwin squeezed the trigger of his Bren. The two soldiers were cut down in a hail of automatic gunfire.

But that gunfire echoed far into the distance, up the ramps they had come, and through the doorway inside. They looked at each other, knowing the element of surprise was gone.

"Come on, let's go!" Burr shouted.

The officer leapt enthusiastically in through the doorway and into a tunnel just three metres wide. Steel ribbing supported the thick concrete walls, and they could tell that nothing below the surface had been affected by the bombing. It was buried too deep and was far too strong.

"How the hell are we gonna blow this place?"

"We'll find a way, Lieutenant," replied Beyett. He rushed in behind them and carefully studied the walls.

"Our demolitions expert," added Corwin.

"I thought you were the medic?"

"I'm a lot of things, but don't you worry about that."

A klaxon style alarm suddenly fired up, and now they knew they truly were up against it. Burr led them on.

"We really have no idea what is being built here, do we?" Corwin asked Beyett.

"Whatever it is it can't be good."

Two soldiers leapt out from a side door ahead and began firing the second they were visible. Both wore the advanced body armour and had assault rifles like those they had seen at Bossan's house. Burr let out a cry of pain and dropped his weapon as he was hit. Corwin and Beyett returned fire, but the two soldiers quickly ducked back in for cover. Corwin kept firing bursts, holding the Bren in one hand and firing from the hip to keep them down. He wrenched out a grenade, pulled the pin, and launched it down the corridor.

It slid to a halt right beside the doorway, and the German soldiers hauled the door shut as the charge exploded. Corwin rushed forwards to discover the steel door barely damaged by the blast, and he could hear the locks being clamped shut the other side. He looked to Rane and he smiled, for he knew exactly what to do. He slipped the Vickers onto his back and rushed at the door, hitting it like a charging bull. The British soldiers once again could not believe their eyes as he struck and barrelled his way through. As he did so, he took hold of the doorway and rushed forwards, using it as a shield as the two soldiers fired. The shots ricocheted from the huge plate of steel, and there was no stopping him. He smashed into them like a freight train. The two soldiers were launched back several metres against the far side wall and crumbled down dead, their bodies broken from the massive trauma.

"You know we tend to use explosives for that, old boy," Burr said to Corwin.

Corwin smiled, for the young Lieutenant sounded like an old man to him. His Sten gun was back in hand. Blood was seeping from a wound on the Lieutenant's upper left arm, but he was ignoring it in a stiff upper lip sort of way.

"And plenty of times, brute strength really is the answer, Lieutenant."

Burr shook his head. "Hard to argue with that."

He carried on along the corridor, and they stopped at a doorway. It had warning signs all over it in German that the contents were highly explosive. They stepped inside to ammunition crates the size of a jeep and stacked to the ceiling. Corwin stepped up beside the nearest one. He drew out his knife and slipped it inside the lid to prise it open. Inside was a warhead that filled the entire container.

"This must be what we came for," said Burr.

Corwin looked up; the crates were stacked as far as the eye could see. Beyett was already studying what was before him.

"Can we set these off with the explosives we have?" Corwin asked.

"Definitely."

"Set three charges here," said Burr.

To their side were two large wheeled trolleys, supposedly designed to transport the warheads.

"Let's take a couple along with us."

Rane wrapped his arms around the first box and hauled it onto the trolley. Nylund and Porter loaded the next.

"Hell, yes," Porter said, marvelling at the huge ordnance he held in his hands, "What I wouldn't give to take a few of these babies home."

The charges were placed, and they were once again heading down the access tunnel they had first started on. It opened out into a vast open plan facility, with missile launch bays set up in rows fifty deep for as far as they could see.

"My god, they don't do anything by half measures, do they?" asked Burr.

Many of the warheads were already mounted in place aboard missiles inside the bays and stacked beside them.

"They must be days away from unleashing these," said Beyett, "Everything here is high explosive, so we cannot risk firing a single shot."

Corwin shook his head. That was not a nice thought.

"Fix bayonets! Nobody pulls the trigger, no matter what!" Burr gave the order.

"You've got to be fucking kidding me," replied Nylund.

"This is gonna be a party," added Porter.

Corwin slipped his Bren gun onto his back and drew out his knife. It was a bizarre situation, for all the lights were on and there was perfect visibility.

"Come on, let's get these charges set," added Burr.

They moved up to the first metre thick support beam, stretched up to the ceiling, and began placing charges.

"You sure these warheads will blow up if we rig them to go?"

Corwin looked back to Beyett to answer the Lieutenant.

"Trust me, they'll go up more easily than you think they can. It'll be a miracle if we are able to get out of here alive."

They continued onwards along the silos placing all the charges they had, but Corwin raised his hand to bring them to a sudden halt. He'd heard footsteps in the distance. He began creeping forwards, leaving the others behind, and still carrying nothing in his hands but his combat knife. He reached the end of a row of missile bays when suddenly someone leapt around the corner and held him at gunpoint. But he sighed in relief on seeing it was one of their own, and Williams was standing just behind him.

Before either of them could say a word, they heard a single Sten gun open up on full auto. It was coming from Corwin's right side, and they knew it must be the Third Platoon at the entrance to the silo.

"What is it?" Williams saw the look of horror on

Corwin's face.

"Look around you. One stray bullet and we could all go up!"

Corwin then rushed towards the sound of gunfire. He took a bend and found the platoon at a broad entrance. It seemed they had been chased into the room and were firing out around a ninety-degree bend.

"Hold your fire!" Corwin hollered.

A few more shots rang out as he shouted it once again, finally grabbing hold of one of the shooters and pulling him back out of view of the enemy.

"Nobody, I mean nobody fires a shot!"

The man looked at him in surprise, but Williams soon appeared and confirmed the order.

"What are we supposed to fight with, Sir?" asked the soldier.

"Bayonets, your bare hands, anything you have to. Even a ricochet could end us all, and they know it. Or why else do you think they aren't firing back?" added Corwin.

The man nodded in agreement and drew out his bayonet.

"Hold this position," he said to the platoon leader and turned back to his people.

They heard a war cry from several soldiers rushing down the corridor with bayoneted rifles. Corwin jumped into the opening and beside one of the rifles and smashed the back of his fist into the man's head. The force stopped his upper body dead, as his legs were thrown forwards, and he went crashing down to the ground. Before he had time to recover from the stunning strike, Corwin stamped on his neck and crushed his windpipe. He proceeded to throw his knife at another soldier, and it embedded in his collar just above the neckline of his body armour.

Corwin leapt forward and drew out the blade, thrusting it back into the windpipe as the man staggered back, and finally slumping down dead. It was all the display of close quarters the British soldiers needed to get the idea. The one he had grabbed placed his Sten gun over his shoulder and drew out a slender stiletto bladed knife from a concealed pocket at his right knee.

"Two minutes to finish setting charges, and then we're out of here," said Williams.

They split up and began planting all the explosives they were carrying. But as Corwin placed his last one, he heard a crashing sound, as if some part of the room was collapsing. He looked around just in time to see a British para fly through the air from behind, and one of the silos then disappeared from view. He could only have been struck by something of superhuman strength.

Another crashing sound rang out as he heard a deep roar. He rushed to the end of one of the silos and looked on in horror to see the last thing he expected or wanted to see there.

"Robak," he whispered to himself.

The giant genetically enhanced monster was in amongst several of the troops and fighting with nothing more than his bare hands. He grabbed one of the men's helmets and twisted to snap his neck. A straight punch to another sent the poor fellow flying through the air and crashing into a support beam of one of the missile supports. His back broke on impact, and he slumped down to the floor.

Williams went at the towering Robak with a bayoneted Sten gun. He ducked under a punch from the creature and thrust the tiny blade into his stomach. But Robak simply placed his hand on the Colonel's chest and shoved him. He couldn't hold onto the weapon and was thrown back onto his back and slid across the floor. Robak pulled out the Sten and tossed it aside as the stunned Colonel drew out his last defence, the same stiletto bladed Fairbairn Sykes knife that they all carried. It seemed to be of little hope against the unstoppable power of Robak.

He stormed towards the Colonel just as he got back to his feet. Williams thrust forward with his knife, but was parried with ease. Robak was just about to deliver a skull crushing punch to Williams' face when Corwin flew at Robak seemingly out of nowhere. He tackled Robak at the waist and struck at a sprint that was enough to knock him aside. It smashed him against the frame of one of the missile bays, and he lost his grip on Williams as he did so.

Corwin stepped back and squared off against Villiers' henchman who looked in utter shock and surprise to seem him. It was obvious that he recognised Corwin, and Rane and Porter appeared at his side a second later. Robak was shaking his head in disbelief, and that made Corwin smile. He now knew that Villiers had no idea of their existence in this time zone.

"Didn't think we'd let you off that easily, did you, Robak?"

He looked to Williams who had gotten the wind knocked out of him and was still staggered by the power and ferocity of Villiers' creation.

"Get your people out of here, Colonel. We'll handle this."

Williams nodded gratefully, slowly got up, and limped off in agony. He headed back to the others and met Burr heading towards him and right to where he had just come from.

"Time to get the hell out of here, Lieutenant."

"Sir, you go on. Captain Corwin and his squad are part of my platoon, and we don't leave them behind."

Williams could see there would be no convincing him otherwise and nodded in appreciation for his efforts.

"Good luck to you, Lieutenant, and God's speed may I see you back in England."

Burr rushed onwards with the eight men of one section he had brought him with. They took the bend and found a monumental battle ensuing.

Robak punched Porter in the face and split his lip. Blood burst out, but Porter quickly returned with a hard strike of his own. Corwin leapt in with a knee into the creature's flank with such immense power that he buckled slightly. Harland was next with a swift forward kicked that knocked the creature back, and Rane rushed at him, as usual like a raging bull.

Rane was only a little smaller than the freakish stature of Robak, and he struck him off his feet and toward a large pane of reinforced glass. The two barrelled through the pane and dropped through the other side. Glass burst out of the floor as they vanished from view. Corwin rushed to the opening; horrified to see it opened out into some type of small underground hangar.

Rane lay flat on the ground fifteen metres below. He was moving, but only barely, and there was no sign of Robak. Without another thought, Corwin, Harland, and Porter jumped from the opening, landing smoothly on the ground beside their wounded friend. Burr rushed to the broken window and looked down at the distance with trepidation.

"Sod that," he said to himself.

He looked to one side and saw a doorway to some stairs.

"Follow me!" he shouted to his own section. Meanwhile, the rest of Corwin's team leapt through to join him.

Corwin was immediately at Rane's side and hauling him onto his feet. He looked stunned and sore.

"Not quite what you were expecting?"

Rane shook his head and winced in pain. Corwin looked up; there were several bizarre looking aircraft beside them, including a giant flying wing aircraft with six jet engines. It looked way ahead of its day.

They suddenly heard the whirl of engines, but it wasn't the prop planes they had encountered so far. This sounded powerful like the jet engines they could see on the flying wing. Then from behind the cover of another aircraft a small twin jet engine fighter appeared.

Corwin reached for his Bren gun because he could see Robak crammed into the cockpit. But the aircraft accelerated at such speed it rocketed past them and out towards the light at the end of the tunnel. Before they knew it, he was gone, and none of them could do anything about it.

"What on Earth was that?" Burr asked, arriving out of breath at Corwin's side.

"Doesn't matter right now, Lieutenant."

"No. We've got four minutes until the first charges go up. We've got no wings and probably no time to get out."

Corwin looked to the opening at the end of the underground landing strip and then back to the huge flying wing that was almost the wingspan of the tunnel.

"Can anyone fly that?" he asked.

Burr looked mortified. "No way. You can't be thinking

we could do that?"

"Improvise and overcome, Lieutenant. That thing must have the payload to carry us all, so again, can anyone fly it?"

"I can," replied Tano confidently.

"No bullshit?" Corwin asked.

"You bet I can!"

"You better be sure, or we're all dead."

"We're all dead if we don't try, Nylund," replied Corwin, "Even if we can get out of the facility, there ain't no easy way out of this country."

He grabbed Rane's arm and placed it over his shoulder, and helped the wounded soldier towards the bizarre looking aircraft.

"Not gonna be a lot of cockpit space in this thing," said Tano.

"We'll use the bomb bays," Beyett said as they opened the side door. It revealed another loading bay to where a substantial payload would be carried.

"Inside!" Corwin ordered everyone.

All but him, Burr, and Lecia loaded up. They shut the doors as Tano and Beyett leapt into the cockpit and tried to get the aircraft up and running. Finally, the other three jumped in, and Lecia pulled the hatch shut behind them.

"This isn't the most solid plan in the world, Captain," said Burr, "We don't even know if this thing flies."

"We'll know soon enough."

Tano looked over all the controls to familiarise himself with them, and finally began pressing switches. To their joy and surprise, the engines fired up.

"How do you know how to fly this?"

Tano looked back at Corwin with an expression of

irritation.

"All right, okay, I don't want to know."

Tano began to put the power down and taxi them into position, and then put down everything they had. They soared forwards and burst out into the open air. Burr was still shaking his head in disbelief that they had even lifted off the ground as they soared into the sky and banked hard.

"Woohoo!" Corwin screamed in ecstasy.

The airy cockpit was filled with glass, and they could see out with great visibility. As they gained height and turned north, they could see flashes of light and fire as the charges blew and the missiles in the silo exploded. Eruptions burst out all across the facility. Holes were ripped through the roof of the structure until finally it shook and buckled under its own weight, and collapsed in on the underground site.

Burr was still shaking his head.

"We really did it."

"Fuck, yes," replied Corwin.

He looked over to Beyett who was breathing heavily. It was clear he'd had no confidence in their ability to get out alive.

CHAPTER ELEVEN

The jet-powered wing had long passed the slower C47 Skymasters while they flew towards the landing strip where they had first left from.

"You know how this is going to look?"

Corwin wasn't sure what Beyett meant and gestured with his hands.

"An advanced German bomber heading towards a military Allied target?"

"Just one aircraft? How much of a threat can we be?"

"Clearly you've never heard of the Enola Gay," replied Tano.

"Should I have?"

Beyett only nodded in agreement. "Do we have any means of communicating with the ground?"

Burr looked over at the limited radio equipment and tried to make sense of it. But he couldn't make head nor tail of it.

"Even if I could get this working, it isn't likely to work on our frequencies, and I don't have any of the calling codes. We need one of the pilots for that."

"This thing is faster than anything the Allies have. We'll just get to the ground and worry about it when we get there."

"Can you even find the airfield?"

Tano looked back with disgust that Corwin even doubted him.

"And land a fast jet on the same strip as those prop planes use?" asked Beyett.

"I gave you a solution. Don't give me problems."

Burr sat back and relaxed as best he could, because he knew there was nothing more he could do. He began to think over all that he had seen that night and then turned to Corwin with a hundred questions in his mind.

"You're not quite human, are you?"

"Well, we are not from another planet."

"But you are not human like the rest of us. You can do things no man could ever do. So what are you, some kind of super soldiers?"

Corwin nodded slowly.

"I don't want to know how or why, just tell me you are here for the right reasons."

"And what are those?" Lecia asked.

"To win this war. To save our country, and the free world before it's too late."

Lecia smiled at his idealistic values.

"Then yes. That is what we signed up for, and that it what we will strive to achieve while we still survive," replied Corwin.

"This is going to be a little tight," said Tano.

"I thought you said you could do this?"

"I can, Boss. Just don't expect it to be pretty."

He reduced their speed in every way he could as they neared the landing strip. They were precisely on target, but coming in at a rapid approach. Only Lecia seemed to be enjoying the adrenaline rush. They touched down and bounced just a little before once again landing on the bumpy strip, but they were still speeding along its length at increasing velocity. Tano began to apply the wheel brakes, and their speed reduced heavily, but they were quickly running out of strip. Finally, he put them on full and locked the wheels.

They could hear the screeching wheels burn rubber, and they slid down the last few metres of the landing strip; at last coming to a standstill just four metres from the grass beyond. Burr gave out a sigh of relief when Corwin was quick to get the door open.

"Nice work," he said to Tano as he climbed out.

"My pleasure."

They opened the payload doors to let the others out. They were all glad to be on firm ground once more. But they could hear vehicles approaching.

"Everybody stay put!" Burr ordered, now realising how suspicious they would look. They all stood out in the open before their aircraft, Corwin and his Luckers, and the few men Burr had brought with them. Two trucks raced into view with a jeep also. Light machine guns were mounted in tandem on the trucks, and troops began pouring out the back.

"Don't move!" one of them shouted as they approached with weapons held at the ready.

Burr shook his head. "RAF Regiment," he said in disgust.

That meant nothing to Corwin, and he didn't like having

several dozen rifles trained on him. He looked around; his people were becoming increasingly anxious.

"Stay calm," he said smoothly.

"Lay down your weapons!"

He was a young Sergeant who looked entirely confused by the whole situation.

"I am Lieutenant Burr of the 7th Parachute Battalion!"

The troops approached them with great caution and suspicion. They almost believed the Lieutenant, until they looked to Corwin, and then the women of the group. They studied the plane once again and could clearly see the German markings on the fuselage.

"You got to be pretty stupid to land a German aircraft here and claim to be friendly," said the Sergeant.

"Yeah, we might have tried a little harder were we the enemy," Porter snapped sarcastically.

"Lay down your weapons!" yelled the Sergeant once again.

"Fuck this shit," replied Porter.

He stepped forward aggressively in spite of the weapons pointed at them, but Corwin thrust out his hand and stopped him dead in his tracks.

"Be cool," he snarled.

They heard another vehicle approaching. It had the distinctive quiet gasoline engine and whirring fan of a jeep. As it came into view, they could see there was just one man aboard, the driver, and it was Hotwell. Corwin felt relieved as he watched the Captain leap out and rush to the Sergeant's side. He looked first to Corwin's people to see they were okay, and then marvelled wide-eyed at the aircraft. He turned to the Sergeant.

"What appears to be the problem here, Sergeant?" he

asked in a confident tone.

The Sergeant lowered his rifle slightly as if doubting himself now.

"Sir, these men...and women...have landed here aboard an enemy aircraft. They are not recognisable as His Majesty's forces or any ally of ours."

"They're American," Hotwell snapped, "But more specifically, they are under my command, and of Colonel Williams of the 7th Parachute Battalion."

"But..."

"But nothing, Sergeant. Your diligence in securing this area is appreciated, but in this matter you are entirely wrong. These are our people. Lower your weapons immediately!"

The Sergeant looked over and signalled to his people. They did as ordered. Hotwell couldn't resist but step up to the aircraft and gaze at its design. He ran his hands along the fuselage and studied the jet engines. He was shaking his head in astonishment.

"You were sent to blow up a facility, and you come back with this...whatever is. How?"

"We needed a ride," replied Corwin with a smile.

Hotwell turned back to the RAF Sergeant.

"Get this aircraft somewhere secure. Inside and under cover, whatever you need to do. I want it out of sight before daylight, you hear?"

"Yes, Sir."

"Trucks are at the far end of the field. We'll see you back at base!" Hotwell shouted, and then beckoned for Corwin and Burr to join him.

"Wow, he really is taking this officer shit seriously," said Porter.

"Whatever rank they give him, he's still our boss,"

added Chas.

"For now. But this is bigger than us," replied Beyett, "We've been left to run free so far. That won't last."

"Why?"

"Because Villiers knows now, Hunter. Knows that we are here, or will do very soon. The whole world will be sure to know about us before long."

"And that's a bad thing?" Porter asked.

"People don't like what they can't understand. We could be seen just as much as the enemy to Allied Commanders as that monstrosity Robak."

* * *

"Colonel wants to see you!"

Corwin woke up as he heard the words. They'd had just a few hours' sleep, but the light of day was piercing through the windows beside him. He groaned, as he got up still mostly dressed from the night before. He pulled on his boots and followed the Captain.

"What's up?" he asked.

Hotwell shrugged. "I don't know for certain, but I am guessing the Colonel is more than a little keen to know how you made it out of there. He only found out an hour ago that you are alive and on the base, and that craft you brought, well. It was snatched away before he could even set his eyes on it."

They arrived at the Colonel's office to find him leaping out of his chair as they went through the door. He was shaking Corwin's hands and patting him on the back.

"Well, Captain, what can I say? We couldn't have done it without you, and I wouldn't have made it out of there alive either without you."

Hotwell looked impressed. He had not heard any of the exploits from the night before, only seen the evidence they brought back.

"Don't you know, Captain? Corwin outdid himself last night. Our operation can be called nothing but an outstanding success. The loss of one aircraft marred the opening of the operation, and has led to losses beyond what I would have wished for. But we got the majority of our boys home. We destroyed the missile facility, and even came home with a rather nice trophy."

"About that aircraft, Sir..." Hotwell began.

"It is already out of my hands. There are minds far greater than ours that will need to spend many hours poring over the wonders of technology that I am told it holds. How on earth you ever flew it is a mystery to me. Your air crew flew out with us."

"My team are trained in a great many things, Sir."

"Evidently so, Captain!"

Williams took a deep breath before getting a weight of his shoulders.

"Captain Corwin, I have provided you with all that you asked, and you have indeed been a boon for this Battalion. We are all thankful for your support, but your exploits last night, and most significantly the seizing of said enemy aircraft, has drawn some attention from over my head. I'm afraid it is out of my hands."

"What are you saying?"

"The Brigade CO is on his way. Brigadier Dorey. He wants to thank you in person and meet the team who snatched an enemy secret right from under their noses, and while completing an essential mission, no less."

Corwin looked back to Hotwell, who only shrugged, for there was nothing he could do.

"Sir, the identity and purpose of my team must remain top secret," insisted Corwin.

Williams nodded.

"As I said, these events are just out of my hands, Captain, and the Brigadier will have more than a few questions if he finds you un-cooperative. Let's face it; you're off the books and more than a little unorthodox in everything that you do. I can accept that, if you can accept that you may have to appease a few people from time to time."

"And completing missions, killing the enemy, and bringing back valuable technology is not enough?"

Williams laughed.

"The Brigadier will merely want to shake your hand and revel in the success that you have brought him. This Battalion, and therefore his Brigade, is the talk of Whitehall right now. Please Captain, run with this."

Corwin finally groaned and reluctantly agreed with the Colonel. There was a knock on the door.

"Ah, here he is now," added Williams with a beaming smile.

Shit, thought Corwin.

He knew they had bullshitted their way through so far, but he had been caught off guard, and by someone in a position of real power. The doors were thrown open as they all leapt to their feet, and the Brigadier stepped in. He was an unusually tall man, a little taller than Corwin, but of slight build and in his mid fifties.

"Welcome..." began Williams.

"Is this the man who stole that fabulous aircraft from right under the Nazis' noses?" interrupted the Brigadier.

"Yes, Sir," replied Williams.

Brigadier Dorey stepped up to Corwin and studied him from head to toe. His stubble and several items of non-regulation kit raised an eyebrow, but he refrained from bringing it up.

"You know when Williams told me he was taking a group of Americans on that mission, I questioned his reasoning, but I could not have been more wrong. You look like you've been a fighting man a lot longer than your country has been in this war, Captain."

"All my life, Sir," he replied.

"I would very much like to inspect your team."

Corwin opened his mouth to speak, but Williams got in ahead of him.

"They are already formed up outside awaiting you, Sir."

Corwin was not impressed, but he knew he had to go along with it.

"Lead the way, Captain," said Dorey.

He begrudgingly got up and did so. They stepped outside to find his squad were formed up for inspection, and not one of them looked happy about it. They stood casually in line and were in a mix of clothing that made them appear the ragtag bunch they were. The Brigadier stopped dead at the first sight of them.

"This is really the team you took with you, Colonel?" he asked Williams.

"Yes, Sir, they may appear a little rough around the edges, but there are no soldiers I would rather have by my side when the shots start flying."

"And women? You take women into combat? And your country allows such a thing? I have never heard of it."

"Not typically, but we are no ordinary outfit, Sir,"

replied Corwin.

"Then what exactly are you?"

"A specialist team, with a broad set of skills."

"In what exactly?"

Corwin shook his head. "Sir, I must emphasise the importance of secrecy in our operations. We are far more than the sum of our numbers, and we can achieve what you would need hundreds, if not thousands to do. We do things our way, and we get results."

Dorey nodded, not quite sure what to make of it all.

"Well, then, while you get results like this, I suppose I can live with the oddities of your team. Keep it up, Captain!"

With that, he turned and left. He climbed into a staff car and was driven away without another word.

"I'm sorry about that, but we must all answer to somebody," said Williams.

Corwin turned to the Colonel with a look of exasperation on his face.

"We might wear your uniforms, but my people are not for you to mess with and drag around like toy soldiers on parade."

"I think you forget to whom you are talking to..."

But Corwin stepped closer into his personal space in an intimidating fashion.

"No, you forget, Colonel. You forgot what our arrangement was. I promised to help you in any way I could, but that doesn't make any of us yours."

Williams nodded; thinking back to how Corwin had saved his life, and that alone was enough for him to back down. Corwin turned to leave, but the Colonel called him back.

"That was fine work last night, and it warrants a celebration. None of us get much to look forward to in life in these times, and we all need something. Be sure you come along. You are already heroes to us."

Corwin gave barely a nod and left.

"A party? There is too much to be done," Beyett appealed.

"Got to learn to let go," replied Porter, happily thinking about the prospects of a late night celebration.

* * *

Three days later.

The sun had long gone down as they lay about their bunkroom. Half of the Luckers were huddled around a table playing a game of cards while the others were scattered about the room. Corwin sat alone with a bottle of whiskey by his side and smoking the cheap ration cigarettes. They passed the time, even if they did taste foul. Lecia approached and sat down beside him but said nothing, as if expecting him to initiate a conversation with her.

"Slow isn't it?" she finally asked when he did not respond.

Her voice was slightly slurred from the amount she had drunk, and she swayed a little in a manner that was unlike her usual precise self. He smiled at the irritatingly vagueness of the question.

"What is?"

"Everything. Were we back home; we would be darting around the world getting shit done. But here we wait and plan, and scheme, and try to lie our way through it all."

"What's your point?"

"That every single day goes by, the less Villiers even matters."

Corwin looked at her and scowled, trying to understand what she meant. Villiers had been all that was on his mind since long before they arrived.

"How can it ever be anything but vital?" he asked her.

"From what Beyett says this is not even close to the way things should be. The Nazis are winning. Villiers might have provided some of the information and tools to get them this far, but say he died tomorrow, has he not done enough already?"

Corwin laid his head back to rest and think about it. He felt her snatch the whiskey from his hands, but he made no attempt to stop her. He knew exactly what she meant, and he had felt it himself, but tried to ignore the fact and focus on their mission to take Villiers down.

He looked over and noticed tears running down her face as she threw back the bottle. It was the first time he had ever seen it, and it shocked him to the core. She had never been anything but confident and resilient to everything that had been thrown at them. He didn't understand it.

"What's wrong?" he asked quietly, so as to not alert the others. Although he could see Frasi at the other end of the room could hear every word.

"We almost had a chance. It was so close, in the palm of our hands. It's a cruel fate that it was snatched away from us, and now we face a life ten times as difficult as the last."

"A chance at what?"

"Peace," she said through the tears.

She lay her hand down on his thigh and looked deep

into his eyes. It spoke far more than her words and struck deep to his heart. It had never even crossed his mind that it was ever a possibility, or that any of his squad would desire it so much. Their training and their enhancements were intended to make them unstoppable war machines that could forgo unnecessary emotion, but it now seemed that had been more effective on some than others.

"What would we even do without a war to fight?"

"I have no idea, but I'd have liked the chance to find out."

Corwin opened his mouth to respond, but before he could get a word out, they felt the floor beneath them shake, and an immensely loud crack and explosion. The windows burst in on them. The tapes reduced the amount of shatter, but Corwin still felt a large shard brush past his cheek and cut him slightly as he dropped to the ground. Several other large explosions rang out nearby.

"What the hell is going on?" Nylund shouted.

"It's an air raid you, asshole!" Porter yelled.

"Everyone stay down!" Corwin ordered.

He crept to the doorway. The door itself had broken off its top hinge and was jammed open. He looked out; bombs were exploding all over. Five bodies lay scattered outside the structure where they had been caught by surprise. Fires were already raging in the main building. Their humble quarters were on the fringe of the base, and so they were having it easier compared to much of the rest.

"We can't stay here!"

"We go out there, and we'll be blown apart, Beyett," said Rane.

"What are you, a pussy?" asked Porter.

They looked to Corwin for answers. He could see the base was being engulfed with flames, and it only appeared to be getting worse.

"No, we can't stay here."

"At least we have a little shelter here," said Vi.

"Yeah, and that ain't gonna do shit when one of those bombs comes through the roof. Go as light as you can," he said, grabbing his Colt pistol from his bed.

He then stepped back to the doorway ready to leave. He peered around the corner to the edge of the base where woods stretched out beyond the outer fence.

"We're going for the tree line, as fast as you can, okay everyone?"

He turned back to the door, but a soldier pushed through and into him. It surprised him for a moment, and he lifted his pistol to shoot, only to realise it was Hotwell. His clothing was cut up at the shoulder, but he seemed relatively unharmed, though he was in total shock.

"Stick with me. Just follow me!"

He nodded, but he was dazed and aloof. Corwin slapped him across the face.

"Hey, stick with me!" he yelled again.

He looked back to the others who were ready to go. Most of them had just a side arm, but Rane was holding on dearly to his Vickers machine gun, and Lecia had her rifle slung on her back. Corwin grabbed Hotwell's arm.

"Go!" he screamed at him.

He rushed out the door and ran as quickly as he could towards the fences. Explosions seemed to trace their footsteps as they hunkered down low. Rane was at the front and crashed into one of the fence posts. It snapped at the base and collapsed before him. They rushed on into the cover of the foliage. Finally, they stopped and ducked down to watch the devastation that they had fled from.

The carnage went on for another five minutes when at last they heard an aircraft sweeping in low. It buzzed overhead at little more than fifty metres above them. It was a single prop engine fighter.

"They've seen us," said Nylund in a panic.

Corwin watched carefully, and the aircraft banked as it went past. Even though he lost sight of it in the darkness of night, he knew exactly what the pilot's intentions were. He looked over to Rane and signalled for him to prepare. He took a few paces forward and waited as the sound of the bombings faded away.

They heard the sound of the fighter approaching from the same direction as before. Just as it came into view, Rane pushed the trigger, and the Vickers exploded into life. Its slow and monotonous rate of fire thumped out the .303 rounds. A few shots hit the ground around him, but Lecia watched the aircraft through her scope, and a hail of gunfire from Rane hit it. The volley ripped through the engine and fuselage. A fire broke out, and the fighter banked hard, going into a dive and crashing out of sight. A burst of flames arose from the crash to light up the night sky, and then there was silence.

* * *

Daylight had finally arrived, and they walked through the wreckage of the base in astonishment. Two thirds of the buildings had been reduced to rubble, and bodies were still being drawn from the rubble. Hotwell was white with shock.

"This was all because of you, because of us, wasn't it?" he asked, his voice ragged.

"A whole fucking war going on, and it's our fault when we get bombed?"

"No, he's right, Vi."

"How'd you figure that, Boss?" Chas asked.

"Because Villiers knows we are here now. Because this target is of no strategic value to the Germans, unless they knew we were here. This was an attempt to take us out before we could put any more spanners in the works."

"I never wanted this," said Hotwell.

"No one did, but there is a price in war. No one wants to pay it," added Corwin.

"Easy for you to say, you lost nothing in this."

Several vehicles were approaching, and one was Dorey's personal car.

"The Brigadier will want answers," said Hotwell. He sounded very worried.

"You made it!"

They turned to see Colonel Williams. He had a bandage running around his head and down his face covering one eye. His left arm was in a support slung around his neck, and there was dry blood across his face and neck.

"All this devastation and you came out of it with nothing to show for it," he stated.

"Are you okay, Colonel?" Corwin asked.

But he only pointed to the approaching vehicles. They watched and waited. But Corwin already knew it wasn't going to be good news. When they came to a standstill, the Brigadier stepped out with a number of MPs at his back. His expression and tone was entirely different to when they last met. He looked confrontational from the moment they saw his face.

"Captain Corwin!"

Corwin stepped forward. He already knew he was not going to like what he was about to hear.

"Captain, this is just enough. We both know that this would never be a target of the Luftwaffe unless there was a major strategic target here. Nothing has changed here recently, except for you!"

Corwin remained silent and waited, although he was trying to understand whether the attack was intended to kill them, or just alienate them from their allies, which was the effect it seemed to be having. He shrugged, for he had nothing to say.

"Captain, you may have achieved a valuable victory for us, but this price, this cost, it goes beyond. No Captain and his squad are worth this. The attack was in your name, so tell me, what is it that makes you people so special to the enemy?"

"It isn't us," replied Corwin in desperation.

"The Nazis want you dead more than almost anything on Earth, why? What are you not telling us?"

Corwin didn't answer him and remained silent.

"Captain Corwin, if indeed that if your name. I have scoured our American contacts for some answers as to who or what you might be. No one has any answers that come close to explaining it. I will no longer go on in good faith with those who cannot be honest with me. If you will not come clean with some real explanation, I will have no choice but to place you under arrest, and assume that you are either spies or independent agents of some nature!"

The Brigadier stood and waited for the response. It was clear he would rather trust them, and have reason to, rather than the alternative, but Corwin could find nothing to say that could be convincing, not after this. He turned and looked to his people. They looked at a loss, and lastly he looked to Beyett in desperation. He wanted to know what to do, but Beyett only nodded to show he must go ahead with what they both knew was the only option. He looked back to the Brigadier and took a deep breath before coming out with it.

"I can be honest with you, Sir, but you will not like the answer."

Everyone there waited with baited breath to hear his story and see the Brigadier's response.

"Give it your best shot, and as all these men as your witness. You will be judged accordingly!" he yelled.

Fires still burned, and bodies were being carried away around them. Corwin knew all hope was lost.

"Sir, you cannot discover our identity, because we are not from this lifetime."

Dorey looked confused, but remained quiet and waited for him to go on.

"As impossible as it might sound, we are soldiers, but from a different war; a war well over a hundred years from now. We passed through some kind of portal chasing the leader of the enemy we faced, and followed that man here."

Corwin fell silent and waited for the Brigadier to answer. He was mulling it over in his head, and he looked far from impressed.

"Time travel?" he finally asked in disgust.

The wounded Hotwell stepped forward in their defence.

"Sir, I must speak for Corwin and his squad, for I have seen…"

"Enough, Captain!" Dorey shouted.

Hotwell looked back to Corwin who only nodded in gratitude and gestured for him to step back.

"Captain Corwin, have you any means to substantiate these ridiculous claims?"

Corwin sighed and shook his head, as he already knew it was now useless.

"I have my word, and the evidence of our work."

"I wish that were enough, Captain. You have cost this Battalion many lives, and you can offer no explanation as to your true nature. I have no choice but to ask that you lay down your weapons and submit to arrest until such time as we can get to the truth of this matter!"

"Fuck that, not again," said Porter.

"Don't you dare fuck this up," Corwin snapped.

But he was shaking his head in disbelief and anger even as he said it.

"It doesn't have to be this way!" he pleaded with Dorey.

"Your choice, Captain!"

CHAPTER TWELVE

"Way to go, landed us behind bars once again," said Porter.

Corwin shook his head and looked around at the room they had been locked away in. It appeared to be an armoury rather than a prison, and all twelve of them were there together. They could hear footsteps approaching, but Corwin didn't get up. He wasn't hopeful of any good news.

Hotwell strode into view. He was still wearing his ripped battledress blouse, and white bandages were visible through the gaps at the shoulder.

"You getting us out of here?" Vi asked.

He shook his head.

"If only I could. But I warned you about sharing wild stories of time travel. It took a lot for me to trust you, an awful lot. It was never going to be any easier with my superiors."

"Even though it is the truth?" Nylund asked naively.

"I will do what I can for you, but things aren't looking good right now. Troops are being mobilised across the country for something big. Most think the Germans will be attempting a major offensive on English soil."

"And we can help," replied Corwin.

Hotwell nodded. "Yes, I know, but it is out of my hands. There's nothing I can do."

"Not good enough, Captain. You know we have a job to do."

"I will appeal to the Colonel and Brigadier Dorey directly, but I do not think they will listen to me."

"You have to try, for all of our sakes."

Hotwell smiled wanly and left, but none of them were hopeful.

"It was worth a shot," said Beyett.

"Really?" asked Tano, "You thought these people would ever believe such an outrageous story?"

Corwin said nothing.

"We are nothing more than freaks to them, just like Robak. We might as well be with the Nazis for all they care."

"Until we prove to them otherwise," said Nylund.

"Your pathetic attempt at chivalrous intent is laughable. Get back to the real world," replied Tano.

A day passed with them behind bars, and they were all becoming more and more concerned. Guards patrolled the building constantly. Corwin and Beyett were anxious of doing any harm to their allies, but they could see several among them were reaching a state where they would do anything to get out from captivity. Corwin watched Porter eyeing up one of the guards and imagining ways of taking him down. The tension in the room was reaching boiling point when Hotwell once again rushed in. He looked even more flustered than the last time.

"What is it?" Corwin asked.

"It's begun!"

"What?"

"The invasion!"

The guards stopped and looked at him in fear as they listened in.

"Seaborne landings all along the southeast coast, as well as multiple reports of airborne operations underway further to the north and west."

"How large?"

"Hard to say, but it's big," Hartwell answered.

"The beginning of the end," said Tano.

Corwin turned to him somewhat confused.

"That is what it was when the Allies did the same."

"What is he talking about?" Hotwell asked.

"In our time line, our history, the Allies launched one of the largest and most ambitious operations in human history. Seaborne and airborne landings in Northern France in June 1944. Hard to imagine how that could ever take place now," replied Beyett solemnly.

"And that was the beginning of the end," added Tano.

"Set us free. Let us help," Corwin begged him.

But Hotwell shook his head.

"I'd be shot for letting you out of here."

"And if you don't, you'll find an enemy bullet soon enough," snapped Vi.

"I'm sorry. I will try and get back to you tomorrow with more news. Maybe the Brigadier will see sense in these desperate days, and realise that you are of more use to us out there than in here."

He turned and left in a state of despair.

"Are we just going to sit around here and do nothing?"

"This is bigger than any of us, Nylund," replied Beyett, "The fight will come to us soon enough."

They fell silent and deep with thought. The silence was suddenly broken by a quiet laugh that got deeper and louder. It was coming from another locked room that they could not see into. It was an eerie sound, and they could do nothing but wait for whomever it was to speak.

"The best soldiers in your army, and here you are, locked in here with me."

They recognised it as the voice of Corporal Winter immediately. Beyett was already shaking his head.

"What the hell is he doing in here?" he asked Corwin, "He is one of the most significant pieces of captured enemy intelligence the Allies will ever know, and they left him here?"

Once again Winter laughed sadistically.

"What is so funny?" asked Corwin.

"That you think you can still fight and win this war. You think you have months or years to keep up this fight, when you only have days. It will soon be over."

Corwin looked to Beyett for answers. "What does he know that we don't?"

"No idea, but clearly we need to find out."

Corwin glanced over to the two guards that were watching them eagle eyed with Sten guns held across their bodies.

"All right, if we do this, nobody dies, you got it?" whispered Corwin.

They all nodded in agreement. He looked to Vi and Lecia and gave them the go ahead. The two women stepped up to the bars of the cells. Lecia drew out a small metal dart hidden in the lining of her coat. She looked back to Vi one last time to check she was ready before launching it with a snap of her wrist. The steel dart struck the one guard between the eyes with the blunt end and knocked him off his feet.

Before he had hit the ground, Vi threw out a fine flexible steel cord that latched onto the submachine gun of the other guard. She tugged back, and he was launched into the bars before her. He tried to wrestle the gun free, but she thrust her arm through the bars and around his neck, pinning him to the cell. He struggled for just a few seconds before passing out.

Rane stepped up to the main door and placed both hands on the bars beside the lock, bent it free, and then heaved the door open. It scraped along the floor from where it had buckled, but could not resist Rane's strength. He rushed to the first guard that Lecia had struck. The man was stunned and trying to regain his senses from lying flat on his back, but the last thing he saw was Rane's fist connecting with his nose and knocking him out cold.

Corwin rushed to the doorway where they had heard Winter's voice coming from. There was a small barred window at eye level on a heavily reinforced doorway. The German Corporal sat at the back of the cell looking completely relaxed and with a smug grin on his face. Corwin took hold of the reinforced frame on the front of the door and tried to pull it open, but he got nothing.

He turned just in time to see Lecia toss him a set of keys from one of the guards. He went through each of the five on the ring, but none seemed to match.

"Guess they really did throw away the key on this one," he said.

"They wouldn't allow guards access to a prisoner this

dangerous," replied Beyett.

"Rane, give me a hand."

"It's no good. You're not getting in. Don't you think I would have been out of here by now if that were the case?"

"We'll see."

"Rane grabbed hold of the door and pulled with Corwin until one of the outer bars buckled slightly, but it had no effect on the structure. Rane pushed Corwin aside and kicked at the lock. There was an almighty crash as his foot landed, but still the door stood as firmly as Winter's smile. But Rane was not deterred. He hit it again, and again, until on the fifth strike the door caved slightly. Winter leapt to his feet and to the side of the cell, realising what was coming next. Rane's foot hit the door one last time, and it was launched off its hinges and smashed into the wall where Winter had been just seconds before. It crashed down to the floor of the cell.

Winter looked genuinely scared now as the towering Rane ducked in through the doorway and stood before him. Corwin stepped inside beside him with Porter taking up the other flank.

"You are going to tell us everything you know," said Corwin.

"Or what?" he asked defiantly.

"Or I leave you to the mercy of him," said Corwin, pointing to Porter who was holding the pig sticker bayonet from one of the guard's Sten guns.

"You'd be amazed what I could do with this," he said with a smile.

"You won't use torture. The noble allies, you would never dream it."

Porter stepped forward with another word and grabbed Winter by the throat. He was strong and tried to resist, but not strong enough. Porter lifted him off his feet and drove the bayonet into his shoulder. The German let out a cry of pain before going limp and stopping his resistance. Porter drew out the blade and dropped him back to his feet.

"I'll never tell you anything," Winter spat defiantly.

"It's gonna be a long night," Corwin replied.

* * *

Captain Hotwell rushed into the former armoury to deliver the news, only to stop dead on finding Harland standing on guard with a Sten gun in hand just inside the entrance of the building.

"How the hell did you get out?"

But no response came. A scream of pain echoed through the halls, and Hotwell hurried on towards the cells. As he got to where he had last left Corwin, he found Winter tied to the top of a table, and the two guards tied to chairs beside him. Winter was covered in blood and heavily bruised from a beating.

"What the hell is going on here?"

Then he recognised the German soldier and shook his head.

"What on earth is he even doing here?"

"A good question," replied Corwin, "I told you how important this man was."

"And I made that clear to the Colonel."

"Obviously not clear enough, Captain."

"Okay, but you can't just torture him. You know what

a crime this is?"

"You know how little that will matter if this country falls?"

Hotwell stood back, but he was far from comfortable with the situation.

"You think torture will get the information you want? A hundred and something years of development and these are your interrogation techniques? It's barbaric."

"You might be surprised how helpful people can be with the right motivation," replied Porter. He then grasped the bayonet that was embedded in the Corporal's shoulder. He began to apply sideways pressure until Winter squirmed, and then punched him in the side of his already badly bruised and bloodied face.

"You're too late to save him," said Winter.

His eyes were rolling, and he looked dazed and barely even awake.

"Save who?" Hotwell asked.

Suddenly the Captain's tone had turned from concern for the prisoner to curiosity and intrigue.

"Your precious Churchill," he said and began laughing as he spat out blood.

Hotwell's face was overcome with a look of terror.

"The Prime Minister?"

When he got no response, he wrapped his hands around Winter's throat and shook him.

"Tell me!"

"He's a dead man, and there is nothing you can do to stop it."

"This is what you were trained for, you and others like you?"

Winter nodded as Hotwell let go his grasp and stepped

back in despair.

"Churchill?" Porter asked.

The name meant little to most of them.

"Only one of the most important wartime leaders of the century," Beyett explained, "Without Churchill to lead this nation, victory may never have been had."

"He is really that important?" Corwin asked.

"You know how important it was to take down Villiers, and still is?"

"It was always our primary mission."

"However important you think it was to victory to take him down, it is just as important for the enemy to end Churchill's life. He is a symbol of resistance in this war. The whole country could come crashing down with his loss," said Hotwell.

Winter laughed once again as blood spewed out onto his white vest.

"This war is already over. You just haven't accepted it yet," he said in spite.

Corwin looked over and lashed out with a rapid back fist into Winter's face that knocked him out cold.

"We could have got more from him," said Hotwell.

"No, we've heard enough. He'll only feed us lies."

"And you are sure this isn't?"

"Pride got the better of him," added Beyett, "I don't doubt that is the truth. And what better time to strike at the country's leader than when the nation's forces are occupied by the greatest threat to this land in hundreds of years?"

"But we have to report this!"

"And who would believe us?" asked Vi, "Last time we tried to help, we ended up in here. There's no chance anyone will listen to a word we have to say."

"What do we do?"

"The only thing we can do, Hunter. The thing we were born and bred to do," Corwin said firmly, "We fight this battle ourselves."

"We are really going to do this? We are going to break out and go for the country's leader? We screw this timing up, and we'll be seen as assassins ourselves," said Vi.

"And we don't try, and it may already be too late."

"What do you want me to do?" asked Hotwell.

"How do we find out where Churchill is?"

Hotwell sighed as began to think about it and then finally came a glimmer of hope.

"Colonel Williams will know."

"You are sure?"

"Absolutely. He's still in a hospital about half an hour from here."

"We cannot use the same methods on an ally," said Beyett.

"No, Williams knows the sort of people we are. I believe he will trust us, and besides it's the only shot we have right now. I can't think of anything else," said Corwin.

He turned back to Hotwell.

"We need transport, and our gear."

"I can get it. It's chaos out there with all this going on. No one will know we have gone for hours. What about him?" he asked, pointing down to Winter.

"Tie him up securely."

"With injuries like that, it could kill him."

"If he dies, he dies," replied Corwin coldly.

A few moments later Hotwell was leading them out and across an open parade ground and into the newer armoury building. He said a few words to the guard and passed through with no resistance at all. All of their equipment was laid out across several racks and tables. But Rane walked past beyond it all and stopped before a massive heavy machine gun lying on a worktop.

"What is that?" he asked.

"Browning fifty calibre machine gun. A fine American weapon that has some vehicle applications, but I can't think you..." replied Hotwell.

But he was silenced as Rane put his hand on the carrying handle attached to the barrel and lifted it off the counter, as if it were little more than an assault rifle in weight.

"Think you can handle that beast?"

Rane nodded to Corwin.

"I hope you know what you're doing. That thing will destroy everything before it."

"Yeah?" Rane asked eagerly.

Hotwell pulled on a set of webbing and began stuffing the pouches with Sten magazines before throwing an additional bandolier of seven onto his back.

"What are you doing?"

"You need me. You know that."

Corwin knew it was true, so he didn't fight it, but he knew the Captain was way out of his element.

* * *

They were on the road once again, and in a single jeep and truck. Hotwell drove the jeep with Corwin next to him.

"When we get there, you let me do the talking, okay? Your people have a tendency to rile people up in a way that isn't all that helpful in these situations."

Corwin couldn't help but nod and smile in agreement.

"You really believe what Corporal Winter was saying?"

"Yeah, because it's what I'd do. You're telling me that if you had even the smallest chance of putting a bullet in Hitler's head, you wouldn't take that chance?"

"It's just not the way we work. It's rather underhand, don't you think?"

"That coming from an intelligence officer? This is war, Captain, not a game."

They pulled up to the hospital and found it was unguarded. Corwin and Hotwell strode inside without a word from anyone. It was a peaceful and quiet facility, but they both knew it would not stay that way for long. Hotwell clearly knew where he was going and led them right to the Colonel's bedside.

"Ah, Captain Hotwell," said Williams as he sat up. But he stopped in shock at seeing Corwin close behind him. Hotwell looked around for a second to check no one was looking. He snapped a quick jab into the Colonel's face and caught him before he fell. He was still conscious but dazed as Hotwell helped him to his feet.

"That's my kind of solution," joked Corwin.

Hotwell sighed.

"I'll be court martialled for it later. Even if we do make this work."

"Cross that bridge when we come to it," replied Corwin.

They passed one of the medical orderlies who looked suspicious.

"Excuse me," began the man.

"Out of the way!" Hotwell ordered.

"Colonel Williams is not fit to leave his bed," protested the orderly.

Hotwell stopped and squared off against the man.

"Don't you know what's going on out there? The Colonel is needed urgently. You'll have plenty more patients to deal with before long. Now stand aside!" he barked.

The man was intimidated and did as he was told as they carried on.

"Nice work," said Corwin.

"You can add that to a long list of shit that is going to be piled on top of my head."

Corwin took the delirious Colonel off his hands when they reached the vehicles, and carefully lifted him into the back of the jeep. He took out his canteen and threw half the contents over Williams' face. He quickly awoke as the cold water felt almost freezing in the cool night.

"What, where?" he asked before he looked at the two of them and remembered.

"Captain Hotwell, you will return this man to his cell immediately."

"No, Colonel, we have a job to do, and we need your help."

"I am not at liberty to help you!"

"Then you condemn your Prime Minister to death," Corwin said.

He opened his mouth to speak, but was silenced by the shock of what had been said. He turned to Hotwell for confirmation, but he only confirmed what Corwin had said.

"A team of highly trained and competent soldiers could well be on their way to assassinate Churchill, even as we speak, Sir."

"And you know this how?"

"Because of Corporal Winter, the man the Germans risked so much to rescue, who has super human strength, and I told you was vital in all of this. The same Corporal you left locked up with us. We got to the bottom of it, but now we have very little time to act."

"And what do you expect me to do about that?"

"You know where the Prime Minister is, don't you?"

"A Battalion commander would not be privy to such information."

"No, but you are, aren't you, Sir?" Hotwell asked.

Finally he gave in.

"I...suppose so, yes. I know where he would be taken at a time like this. But I could never share that information with you, or any one for that matter."

"Colonel, I saved your life, and all I ask now is that you trust me."

Williams grit his teeth and thought it over. He still looked uncertain.

"Time is not a luxury we have right now," added Corwin.

"Don't make me regret this," he replied quietly.

"All right, we need to get there ASAP."

"Then you'll need a plane."

Hotwell immediately fired up the engine and spun the rear wheels as they got back onto the road.

"Are you really sure about this?" Williams asked, as they tore through the countryside.

"Sure enough to be worried, and do whatever is necessary to be there to prevent whatever might go down," replied Corwin.

Williams was rubbing his sore face and then remembered how he had arrived at the vehicle.

"You know if you are wrong about this, Captain

Hotwell, you're going away for a long time.

"Tell me about it," he replied sarcastically.

He no longer seemed to care about his own fate, and that only endeared him further to Corwin.

"You know you don't have to come with us?"

"Yes I do. However this ends, you are going to need someone to pull you out of the mess as usual," replied Hotwell.

They reached familiar roads, and Corwin knew they were being taken back to the airfield they had arrived at in the German bomber. He turned back to Williams in the back.

"We need a plane. We can take it by force, or you can ensure we get it without any harm coming to friendlies, so what's it going to be?"

Williams was shaking his head with uncertainty again.

"How do I know I can trust you?"

"What does your gut tell you?" Corwin asked, staring into his eyes.

He had realised on gut instinct so much in life that he just hoped it would work for someone else now. He could see the Colonel wanted to believe their story.

"An attempt on Churchill's life? I can believe that, but what you said to the Brigadier, that you are time travellers. I find it hard to wrap my head around it. And hard to believe you as a result."

"It's tough to accept, unless you believe that I was telling the truth."

"And you stand by that? It wasn't just some wild story, you really stand by that explanation of who and what you are?"

"I do."

He was still shaking his head.

"Any other day of my life, and I'd call you crazy and tell you to bugger off. But we live in desperate days, and so maybe I am just willing to give you the benefit of the doubt. For now."

"Thank you, Sir."

It wasn't long before they arrived at the airfield and stopped at the main gates. The first face they saw was the Sergeant of the RAF Regiment that had accosted them upon their last arrival.

Ah shit, he thought.

But the Sergeant soon turned his attention to Colonel Williams and waved for the other soldier to raise the gate and let them through without any further questions.

"Wow, that was easy," Hotwell whispered as they passed through and onto the airstrip.

They headed for the nearest hangar where they could see a line of C47 Skymasters.

"We'll need a pilot," said Corwin.

"Don't you worry about that. We've got that covered."

They pulled up beside one of the aircraft that appeared set to go. Several of the ground crew were nearby. They saw the three officers step out of the jeep and didn't say a word.

"This bird fuelled and ready to go?" Hotwell asked.

"Yes, Sir!" a response came.

"All right, load up!" he shouted across to the others.

Corwin's squad began piling into the aircraft.

"Can you fly this?" Corwin asked Tano as he climbed aboard.

"Seriously?"

"We've still got no idea where we are going. No flight

plan, no clearance," said Hotwell.

Corwin shrugged. "Make do, improvise, and overcome."

"I can outline this for you," added Williams. He was slumped beside the wing just off to their flank.

"Oh, no, Colonel, you are with us on this to the very end."

He reached forward and grabbed Williams. He shoved him towards the door where Rane helped him aboard.

"You have to trust us on this one. We also need to trust you, Sir," added Corwin.

The last of them were loading up when they heard two vehicles approaching. Corwin didn't want to appear a threat to whoever it was, so simply turned and waited for who or whatever it might be. Two jeeps rolled into view and stopped before them, and a number of soldiers leapt out to confront them. He could feel his grip tighten slightly on the Bren gun slung over his shoulder, but he knew he had to refrain from using it.

"Captain Corwin?" a voice asked.

He couldn't help but feel they were busted, but then the source of the call stepped info view. It was Lieutenant Burr.

"What can I do for you Lieutenant?"

"Sir, whatever you are doing, and wherever you are going, we want in."

The Lieutenant stood beside eight of his men. Corwin recognised all of their faces. They were all survivors of their mission to destroy the missile silos in France.

"This operation isn't exactly on the books, Lieutenant, or particularly legal."

Burr took a deep breath and smiled.

"Captain, my boys here are confident that whatever

you are doing, it's doing a lot of good. Our Battalion has been smashed. We're getting amalgamated with others in the Brigade. But we are still here, and you are still here. Whatever it is you are planning, it must be important, and we want in."

"And if I told you this is probably the most dangerous and stupidest thing you've ever done?" asked Corwin.

"I'd ask, where we can sign up?"

"Then climb aboard."

They rushed to the door and clambered in, but Hotwell was not happy.

"Don't you think you've caused enough trouble here?"

"Why stop now?" replied Corwin. He climbed aboard and reached down to help the Captain in.

Corwin went past everyone to reach the cockpit where he found the Colonel sitting in the co-pilot's seat.

"You know where you're going?" he asked Tano.

"I've got a pretty good idea."

He fired up the engines, and they were soon on their way. Time seemed to pass quickly when Williams shouted out to him.

"We're coming up on the spot!"

He rushed back to the cockpit. The moon provided some light, but the ground below was in almost complete darkness in blackout conditions.

"Find us someone to put down," said Corwin.

"You don't land these things like a DART, you know."

"Never mind that, just find us somewhere."

They began to bank and after a few minutes Tano had settled on a location. They reduced speed and came in for a smooth landing on a field that proved to be bumpier than they expected. The Skymaster bounced several times before crashing into the soft ground, digging and cutting channels across the field. They finally came to a standstill just a few metres short of a line of trees.

"You're crazy, you know that?"

"Possibly, Sir, but not stupid," replied Tano.

They jumped out of the aircraft and found themselves in complete tranquillity. Corwin had no idea what part of the country they were even in, but it would mean nothing to him, so he didn't bother asking.

He tossed a Sten gun and a bandolier of magazines at the Colonel and added, 'Lead the way."

Any hostility Williams felt had vanished, as he could not help but be endeared to Corwin and his unusual methods.

"We are going to get to the house and find nothing untoward at all," he stated.

"We can hope," replied Corwin.

"We must be about half an hour out," he replied as he quickly surveyed the terrain and set off. They worked their way across farmland and woodland for the whole trip and saw no signs of life at all. Then they broke through some foliage to a clearing, and there was a large manor house way off in the distance. Corwin raised his hand and called them to a halt. He knelt down to survey the scene.

"You see, Captain, do you see anything wrong here?" Williams asked.

He could make out the silhouettes of a number of soldiers patrolling the building and surrounding area. Two armoured cars were parked beside the building and several other cars and jeeps. Corwin shrugged.

"All this way for nothing. So what now? We can't go bursting in there and introduce ourselves. We'd be shot before we get close. I am afraid it might be back to prison for you lot. Might be time to let this go now before you make it any worse."

But Corwin refused to accept that.

"No, we wait. Whatever is happening it is going down tonight."

Three hours went by, and Corwin constantly checked his watch. He knew they were getting close to daybreak, and he was starting to doubt it all, when they heard the roar of engines overhead. Three large prop plane bombers flew in at low altitude, and they could instantly see they were of German design.

"Oh, my god," said Williams.

"They're too low to drop bombs," said Beyett.

They watched dozens of soldiers leap out from the aircraft, but they did not use parachutes. Small jets fired on their backs, and they descended rapidly to the ground, landing in the grounds amongst the soldiers on patrol. It was too far to see for sure, but they looked larger than any normal human.

"Protect the Prime Minister!" Williams shouted, rushing forward, and the others tried to catch up.

CHAPTER THIRTEEN

Corwin quickly caught up with the enthusiastic Colonel when he reached the outer railings. He grabbed the officer by the back and jumped with him so that they both cleared the two-metre obstacle with no effort at all. The rest of Corwin's team followed suit, and the Paras leapt up nimbly to clear them like any normal human would do.

Automatic gunfire rang out as they approached the vast manor house, and one of the enemy fighters was firing some kind of horizontally magazine fed machine gun. But most strikingly of all, the soldier wore a mechanical armoured suit. Thick armour plating covered his back and chest, with lighter plates reaching down his shoulders and thighs. It resembled a primitive and smaller version of the immensely powerful mech suit they had encountered at Villiers' base.

Rifle and submachine gun fired bounced off the armoured German soldier, and he returned fire, cutting down three British soldiers at the entrance to the house. Others ran for cover as more of the mechanised suits advanced without effort. Corwin took aim at the back of the nearest one and fired from the hip with his Bren. The weight of fire caused the soldier to stagger forward slightly, but he seemed unharmed. He turned to return fire, but Rane stopped beside him and squeezed the trigger on his Browning.

The heavy machine gun thundered to life with slow thunderous rate of fire. The huge rounds punched holes through the armour and exited the back of the soldier's rear plate. He was killed instantly.

"I like this!" Rane hollered.

Six of the armoured soldiers rushed in through the front of the house as they opened fire, but it was too late; they had got inside. Gunfire hit the ground around Corwin, and he looked up. Dozens of paratroopers were dropping from the sky. A number were firing sporadically at them as they made their descent. He raised his Bren to the shoulder and took aim.

They wore lightweight body armour and carried assault rifles. Two bursts from Corwin's Bren cut through the groin and into stomach of the one that had been shooting at him. The soldier slumped dead and dropped lifelessly to the ground as his parachute encompassed his body.

"Keep moving!" Corwin ordered.

He kept firing from the hip at the paratroopers landing amongst them. He felt two shots in his back and jolt him slightly, but he made it to the colonnade that led to the main door of the house. He ducked behind the cover of one of the wide columns and slammed a new magazine into his weapon. He raised it up beside the cover and took aim. Most of his team had made it along with him, and the British paras were running amok amongst the German troopers as they fought to get free of their parachute lines and harnesses.

Corwin fired a burst into the face of one and killed him instantly as muzzle flashes lit up the open field before them. Chas was darting in and out of them with a pistol in each hand, as if practicing an elaborate dance rather than fighting. She shot one point blank in the face, leapt over his body, firing into both legs of another, and finally shooting into his throat. She then carried on.

"We've got this. Go!" Vi yelled across to him.

Corwin, Porter, Nylund, Beyett, Hunter, and Williams rushed through the entrance of the house. They found the bodies of three British soldiers at the foot of a lavish double staircase.

"Why would they try and do this by hand, why not just carpet bomb the place and flatten it?" Nylund asked.

"The bunker under this place is rock solid. I'm not sure they'd even touch it. And even if they could, you know how many doubles there are of the Prime Minister? If they are going to kill Churchill, they will need irrefutable evidence that no one in the world would disbelieve," replied Williams.

"Lucky for us," added Corwin.

"We've got company!"

Vi flew through the door firing her Thompson on rapid fire. Gunfire ripped through the doorway and hit one of the paras as they rushed inside. Harland grabbed the webbing of the wounded man and hauled him inside, and they all ducked down for cover.

"If we can hold for long enough, the whole bloody Army will get here. We just have to make sure they don't get to Churchill!"

Corwin agreed with the Colonel.

"Rane, Hunter, Harland, take the east wing. Porter and Lecia, you're with me. The rest of you hold this ground. We'll deal with whatever is inside, but you must hold back any further advances!"

"I'm coming with you," said Williams.

"Okay."

The others smashed out several nearby windows and began laying down fire. He nodded for Rane to go on, and then turned and led the three he had with him to the west side of the stairs and further into the house. They could already hear the gunfire intensify at the entrance they had just left, but Corwin knew he could not afford to be distracted.

They heard the rapid fire bursts of the magazine fed light machine guns they had seen carried by the up armoured German soldiers minutes before, and he knew they must be close. Several Sten guns rattled off shots in the distance but were soon silenced by the relentless advance of the German forces. Corwin took a bend to find they were at the far end of a corridor, with two of the German soldiers facing away and advancing ahead.

Under the lights of the house he could now see better what they were dealing with. The soldiers wore a mechanical suit that extended the length of their body to the ground for load bearing, allowing them to carry far more weight than a human should be able to manage. The armour that covered two thirds of their body looked thick enough to have come from an armoured car.

"Rane sure would be useful right about now," whispered Porter.

But Lecia was not deterred. She raised her rifle and

took careful aim at the rear leg joint and squeezed the trigger. The shot hit one of the shocks on the knee joint and seized, causing the soldier to tumble over like a ton of bricks. As he went down, Porter and Corwin opened fire with repeated bursts from their Bren guns. The soldier spun around as bullets bounced from his armour and revealed he carried a huge breaching shield in his left hand. Dozens of shots ricocheted from its surface, and the man began to run towards them.

"Oh, fuck," said Corwin.

He kept up the fire until his magazine ran dry, and he ducked back to load in another. But the soldier rushed through the doorway and hit Porter square on. He was launched through the air and crashed into a vast mirror mounted over a fireplace three metres from where he'd been standing. The soldier carried a machine gun single handed in his other hand and spun it round to target Corwin. But the Captain released his grip on his Bren and grabbed the receiver and stopped it dead as the soldier pulled the trigger. Automatic gunfire strafed the wall.

He kept his grip with his left hand and drew out his knife, thrusting it deep into the inside elbow where there was no protection at all. The soldier let out a cry in pain from beneath his enclosed face helmet, but quickly lashed out with his shield. The edge of the table-sized slab of steel was thrust into his face, and he felt the impact almost break his jaw and cut his lip open.

He recovered quickly and ducked under the shield, pulling his knife back out from the soldier's arm and thrust up into his groin. The man keeled over with the knife still embedded deep. Corwin took hold of the soldier's helmet in both hands and snapped his neck.

The body slumped heavily to the ground. He caught a glimmer of movement out of the corner of his eye. Lecia was on top of the soldier she had disabled with her first shot. She was holding his arms down with one hand and driving a fine blade into the eye slit of his helmet. He finally went limp. Porter groaned as he got back to his feet.

"What a mother fucker," he complained, as he picked up his weapon.

Williams stepped out from cover where he had stayed out of the vicious struggle. Corwin flipped over the body of the one he had killed.

"Pretty much no armour on legs and lower arms," he said and carried on towards Lecia.

Several explosions rang out that vibrated violently through the floor.

"They must have found the entrance to the bunker," said Williams.

* * *

Harland led the way, and they passed the bodies of several British soldiers. They came across one of the German armoured warriors trying to get back to his feet. His legs and left arm were bloody where he had been hit by submachine gun fire. Harland stepped up to the soldier and placed a foot down on his rifle that pinned it to his body, and he was stuck. He reached down and took hold of the front of the man's helmet and ripped it from his head. The leather strap was torn from its rivets.

He held up the helmet for a second to study it. It weighed as much as the Bren he was carrying, and looked more like something from an age of armoured knights than anything close to a time he knew. He looked down at the soldier to see the man couldn't understand how he could not fight his way free from Harland's grip.

"Come on, we have to keep moving," said Rane. He and Hunter went on.

Harland swung the helmet into the wounded man's face and crushed his skull with a single strike before tossing the helmet aside and carrying onwards. Hunter was in the lead now, and he reached a doorway where he stopped dead as he saw Robak lift up part of a damaged metal trap door and toss it aside.

"Robak!" he screamed.

He lifted up his Bren gun and fired repeatedly from the hip as he rushed toward Villiers' henchman. He wore the same thick steel armour that the rest did, but with no need for mechanical enhancement to support the weight. Bullets bounced from his armour, but he leapt through the hole in the floor without paying any attention to Hunter.

"Stop!" Rane shouted.

He and Harland rushed after the young soldier. Gunfire landed at Hunter's feet as he ran onwards. They reached the doorway to get a full view ahead. Three German soldiers were firing at Hunter, and he jumped and slid along the floor, dropping into the hole unscathed. The Germans turned their attention to them now, but it was too late. Rane opened fire with the Browning and ripped through their armour. Shards of wood and brickwork littered the air. The three soldiers vanished into a haze, and finally he stopped firing. They got one foot forward when they heard an almighty explosion and felt the wall behind them cave in.

They were showered with debris as they ducked down

and sheltered their eyes. As they looked back up, the silhouettes of dozens of enemy soldiers were advancing towards the breach, and they knew they had to try and hold them back.

Hunter landed hard almost ten metres down from where he had slid into the hole. He coughed and spluttered as brick dust filled his lungs, and he got to his feet. He saw a shadow disappear up ahead and heard the heavy footsteps of Robak. He looked back up as if hoping for some help, but it never came, so he ran onwards without any caution at all. Gunfire rang out from a low calibre pistol, and he took the bend to find Robak snap a soldier's spine over his knee before tossing him aside.

He quickly took aim and fired several bursts into Robak. The weight of the rounds was enough to knock him back slightly, but not one penetrated his armour. The huge creature squared off against him and almost filled the narrow corridor. He took one last careful aim for a headshot and squeezed the trigger. He heard a click, as the bolt went forward and found an empty chamber and magazine.

Robak grinned and stood defiantly with no weapon in hand, but Hunter was not deterred. He asked himself what Corwin would do, and he knew immediately. He lifted the sling of his Bren gun off his shoulder and threw the weapon to the ground. He drew out his knife with his right hand and his pistol with his left and ran at Robak. He fired repeatedly until the seven shot magazine was empty. One shot skimmed Robak's neck and cut deeply, hurting him enough to give Hunter the smallest of openings. He dropped the pistol and jumped into the air with his knife aiming for Robak's collar. Hunter landed with his arms wrapped around Robak's chest and his blade running sure and true for its target.

The tip of the blade got to within a few centimetres when Robak's hand flew into view and blocked its path. The blade pierced his palm and ran up to the hilt and stopped short of his neck. He responded with a head butt that sent Hunter hurtling to the floor with blood spewing from his nose and mouth.

Robak drew out the knife and threw it aside as he strode forward. Hunter tried to get to his feet, but it was too late. Robak delivered a swift kick to his flank. Several of his ribs cracked on impact even through his armour, and he was once again launched through the air and landed hard on the cold concrete floor. He spat out blood and winced in pain as he got back to his feet, gesturing for Robak to come forward.

"Come on, just a little longer," he whispered to himself.

* * *

Corwin rushed towards the sound of the Browning gunfire, knowing it could only be Rane. He ran into the room to find the bodies of several soldiers. Rane and Porter were reloading inside a doorway while under heavy fire. He looked down at the hole in the floor where the trap door was.

"Where's Hunter?"

"He went in after Robak!" Porter replied.

"And you let him go alone?"

"Kind of busy here!"

An explosion rang out in the wall a few metres to Porter's side, and a new entrance into the room was created. Lecia and Williams were quick to rush to the breach. They tossed grenades through and returned fire at the oncoming troops.

"We have to get to Robak!" Corwin shouted.

"You do, but if we can't hold back this wave, it won't matter!" Williams answered.

"We've got this, go!" Porter called over to him.

They were barely holding back the waves of German paratroopers and their armoured support troops. The last thing he ever wanted to do was face Villiers' henchman alone once again, but he thought of Hunter, and took the leap. He landed smoothly at the base and raised his weapon ready as he rushed onwards. He took a bend and felt his heart almost stop when he saw Hunter laying lifelessly a few metres ahead.

He rushed to the youngster's side. Thankfully, his eyes were still open, but he could not move any of his body. His breathing was slow, and it was clear his body was completely broken.

"I tried," he whispered as tears mixed with the blood splattered all across his face. Corwin rested his hand on Hunter's cheek.

"You did well."

Automatic gunfire suddenly echoed through the corridor. It was the distinctive sound of a Thompson machine gun firing on full auto. He got to his feet and rushed ahead as quickly as he could. He reached a blast door that had been prised apart. Five bodies were stacked in the entrance as well as another three further in, and then he saw him. Churchill. He stood defiantly in the centre of the room with a cigar in his mouth and a Thompson machine gun in hand. He had on his full uniform and was holding the trigger firmly down and letting out a hail of bullets.

Robak was advancing towards him and taking all the fire without any concern at all as the .45 bullets ricocheted off his armoured suit. The shots continued to fly until his drum magazine ran empty. Robak was just two metres away from him and stopped to gloat.

"Your war is over," he stated.

He strode towards the Prime Minister, but Corwin took a quick aim at the back of his legs. He fired the last two bursts in his magazine, and the shots ripped into Robak's thighs. He screamed in pain and was felled like a wild beast. He smashed down to the floor just in front of Churchill who hadn't even flinched.

"If I may?" Corwin asked him.

He's all yours," replied Churchill, stepping back out of the way.

Corwin entered the room and squared off against Robak as he struggled to get back to his feet. Blood was seeping from his wounds, and Corwin could see he was in pain now.

"Will you never die?" Robak asked.

"Not a chance."

Robak laughed.

"You couldn't beat me before, not without your dogs, how will this end any differently? You will never leave here."

"Yeah, we'll see about that."

Corwin charged forward as if to throw a punch, but stopped short and delivered a quick push kick into Robak's wounds on his right leg. His boot struck hard, and Robak keeled forward slight, allowing Corwin to deliver a powerful uppercut into his broad jaw. Robak's head snapped back slightly, but he threw his hand around with a quick back fist that smashed Corwin by his right ear and sent him staggering several paces across the room before gathering his balance.

Corwin took hold of a steel chair, threw it at Robak, and then rushed at him. He cast the chair aside, but Corwin ducked down and delivered a quick punch to the inside if his right thigh, once again hitting the wound; Robak groaned in agony. Robak thrust a knee forward to strike him, but could not generate the power he wanted through the weakening muscles.

As Robak stumbled slightly from his weak legs, Corwin punched him straight in the throat and cut his air supply off for just a second. He reached for his throat and tried to breathe. Corwin didn't let up. He delivered two jabs and a heavy hook to his nose that weakened him further, and finally leapt over onto his back and took him in a chokehold.

Robak grabbed hold of his arms and stood up even with the weight of Corwin on his shoulders and the injuries to his legs. Corwin felt his feet come off the ground, and Robak reached to punch him in the face. The strike landed, but it was weakened, and he took it. Robak went back a few paces and smashed him against a wall, trying to crush him with his weight, but Corwin held on for dear life.

Finally, Robak slumped onto his knees and collapsed to the floor with Corwin on top of him. Corwin let out a sigh of relief as he got up and drew out his knife.

"You will not harm another soul," he said as he moved the blade towards the unconscious man's throat.

"Why would you kill this man?" Churchill asked.

Corwin was shocked.

"You think I should show mercy after all that he has done?"

Churchill shook his head.

"Mercy? Far from it. Just look at him, and all that he was able to do. You know what we could achieve with an army of soldiers like him?"

Corwin nodded.

"Like him? No, he's a monster, but like me? Yes, Sir."

"A dozen of my finest men were thrown aside like nothing at all, and yet you bested him all by yourself. What are you?"

Corwin smiled. "It's a long story, and you wouldn't believe me, anyhow."

"Try me."

Corwin slowly knelt down beside Robak.

"Well, we don't come from this country, nor this time…" he began, as he rolled over the hulking body and reached in to check for a pulse. Robak was still breathing, and that made him uncomfortable.

"I really wish you would let me…" Corwin began and looked back up to Churchill, but stopped dead at what he saw.

Tano stood beside the Prime Minister with a pistol held to his head.

"What the hell are you doing?"

He couldn't believe what he was seeing. For a moment he began to wonder if it were some kind of trick or imposter.

"You've got this all wrong," stated Tano.

Corwin stood up and began to approach.

"Stay where you are, Corwin," he said calmly.

"Okay, tell me how you think it is."

"The Germans want to kill this man because he presents a threat to them, but isn't this the sort of power we have been in search of since we arrived in this damned place?"

"Not sure what you are getting at," replied Corwin.

"We kill this man, and we can lead this country to victory, or you can squander our abilities and let us rot in another jail cell until Villiers finds us."

"I just don't see it that way," replied Corwin.

"I pull the trigger, and we can start changing the outcome of this war."

Corwin could hear the sincerity in his voice. He was genuinely attempting it for the right reasons, but he couldn't let him go ahead with it. He raised his empty hand and clicked his fingers. A single shot rang out from Lecia, who was just peering through the doorway behind him. Corwin felt the turbulence as the bullet past within millimetres of his ear and struck the slide of Tano's pistol.

As the gun flew from his hand, Frasi seemed to leap out of nowhere and lock Tano into an arm bar and collapse with him to the floor. He landed hard and could not resist the strong lock he had been placed in.

"You know how fucked up that was?" Corwin asked.

Colonel Williams rushed into the room and to Churchill's side. He looked down at Tano having his hands bound by Lecia.

"He is one of yours?"

Corwin turned to the Prime Minister and nodded in shame.

"I want him arrested immediately. He should be shot for this," said Churchill sternly.

"Sir, I must protest," said Williams.

"You were not here, Colonel. This man tried to kill me just like that thing did," he said, pointing to Robak.

"Sir, we've got the situation under control. You are safe now."

"Yes, I should bloody well hope so. Now, about this defector."

"If it were not for him, Captain Corwin and his team would never have made it here. And they are responsible for your life here today. They did this for you."

Churchill turned his attention to Corwin and was starting to understand he was far more significant than his rank might suggest.

"You're a little old for a Captain, aren't you?" he asked.

"Until a few days ago it was Sergeant, but not in your army," he replied.

For a minute Churchill carefully studied Corwin and his ramshackle group of companions. He knew it was perhaps their single opportunity to make their case and really make a difference.

"Women? You fight with women at your side?" Churchill asked, gazing upon the bedraggled beauty of the Lecia and Chas, but passed off the rather more odd looking Vi who glared at him in a way that seemingly no woman ever had before. But it was when Rane stepped into the room that his eyes truly widened.

"I didn't ask for this, and I have no idea who you people are or what you are doing here, so what is it I can do for you?"

Corwin knew he had it in the bag. He pulled out one of the god awful cheap cigarettes and lit it, smiling as he replied.

"It's not what you can do for us. It's what we can do

for you. We're here to turn this war around. All you have to do is let us."

Churchill looked suspicious as he continued to gaze upon the absurdity of everything he was seeing. He looked back down to Robak and remembered the vicious fight that had been displayed before him.

"Any man that can wrestle a giant like that and win is a friend I would be glad to have in this world," he replied.

He strode across the room and took out a tin. He popped it open and pulled out two cigars and passed one to Corwin, offering out his other hand in friendship. Corwin smiled. He knew they were finally in the right place and talking to the right man.

"We've got a war to fight, and no time to sit idle. Will you fight it with me?" Churchill asked him.

Corwin shook his hand and took the cigar with delight.

"Bet your ass," he replied.